BEST LITERARY TRANSLATIONS

Best Literary Translations 2024

JANE HIRSHFIELD, GUEST EDITOR

Noh Anothai, Wendy Call, Öykü Tekten,
and Kọ́lá Túbọ̀sún

SERIES COEDITORS

DEEP VELLUM PUBLISHING
DALLAS, TEXAS

Deep Vellum Publishing
3000 Commerce St., Dallas, Texas 75226
deepvellum.org · @deepvellum

Deep Vellum is a 501c3 nonprofit literary arts organization
founded in 2013 with the mission to bring
the world into conversation through literature.

Support for this publication has been provided in part by grants from the National Endowment
for the Arts, the Texas Commission on the Arts, the City of Dallas Office of Arts and Culture,
the Communities Foundation of Texas, Anaphora Literary Arts, the Marin Community
Foundation, and the Addy Foundation.

LIBRARY OF CONGRESS CATALOGING-IN-PUBLICATION DATA

Names: Hirshfield, Jane, 1953- editor.
Title: Best literary translations 2024 / Jane Hirshfield, guest editor.
Description: Dallas, Texas : Deep Vellum Publishing, 2024. | Series: Best
   literary translations ; vol 1
Identifiers: LCCN 2023054173 (print) | LCCN 2023054174 (ebook) | ISBN
   9781646053353 (trade paperback) | ISBN 9781646053391 (ebook)
Subjects: LCSH: Literature--Translations into English. | LCGFT: Poetry. |
   Short stories. | Essays.
Classification: LCC PN6019 .H57 2024 (print) | LCC PN6019 (ebook) | DDC
   808.80441802--dc23/eng/20231213
LC record available at https://lccn.loc.gov/2023054173
LC ebook record available at https://lccn.loc.gov/2023054174

ISBN (hardcover) 978-1-64605-335-3 | ISBN (Ebook) 978-1-64605-339-1

Cover design by Zoe Norvell
Interior layout and typesetting by KGT

PRINTED IN THE UNITED STATES OF AMERICA

Contents

Coeditors' Introduction   11

Guest Editor's Introduction: In Words and Beyond Them   19

Near the Shrine of Saint Naum   31
Najwan Darwish
translated from the Arabic by Kareem James Abu-Zeid

From *Guerrilla Blooms*   33
Daniela Catrileo
translated from the Spanish by Edith Adams

Hymn to Ra   38
unknown author
translated from the Old Egyptian by Samson Allal

We Will Survive   41
Rolla Barraq
translated from the Arabic by Muntather Alsawad and Jeffrey Clapp

Neighbor   44
Yoo Heekyung
translated from the Korean by Stine Su Yon An

Family Portrait of the Black Earth   47
Yordanka Beleva
translated from the Bulgarian by Izidora Angel

00572   51
Julia Rendón Abrahamson
translated from the Spanish by Madeleine Arenivar

Graceless   57
Samwai Lam
translated from the Chinese by Natascha Bruce

[I have a collection of powerful objects]   69
Jesús Amalio Lugo
translated from the Spanish by David M. Brunson

Death, Peppermint Flavored   73
Ashur Etwebi
translated from the Arabic by James Byrne and Ashur Etwebi

Our Village   76
Tesfamariam Woldamarian
translated from the Tigrinya by Charles Cantalupo and Menghis Samuel

The Sea Krait   80
Enrique Villasis
translated from the Filipino by Bernard Capinpin

A Red Blight   84
Juan Cárdenas
translated from the Spanish by Lizzie Davis

Deterioration   95
Fatemeh Shams
translated from the Persian by Armen Davoudian

Bone   98
Behçet Necatigil
translated from the Turkish by Neil P. Doherty

Rune Poems from Bergen, Norway,
        Thirteenth and Fourteenth Century   100
unknown author
translated from the runic alphabet by Eirill Alvilde Falck

The Funeral   103
Geet Chaturvedi
translated from the Hindi by Anita Gopalan

Settling: Toward an Arabic Translation
        of the English Word "Home"   114
Hisham Bustani
translated from the Arabic by Alice Guthrie

The Lion   121
Farhad Pirbal
translated from the Kurdish by Jiyar Homer and Alana Marie
        Levinson-LaBrosse

Joyful Mythology   129
Zuzanna Ginczanka
translated from the Polish by Joanna Trzeciak Huss

The Snail's Spiral   133
Disney Cardoso (in collaboration with Christian Rincón)
translated from the Spanish by Jeanine Legato

Water_Miniatures: Unboxing   142
Gala Pushkarenko
translated from the Russian by Dmitri Manin

A Body   147
Catalina Infante Beovic
translated from the Spanish by Michelle Mirabella

From *Unstill Life with Cat*   152
Anna Felder
translated from the Italian by Brian Robert Moore

Bottle to the Sea (Epilogue to a Story)   158
Julio Cortázar
translated from the Spanish by Harry Morales

First We'll Speak Many Words About God   166
Almog Behar
translated from the Hebrew by Shoshana Olidort

In the Meantime / Mientras llega   173
Luis Alberto de Cuenca
translated from the Spanish by Gustavo Pérez Firmat

Bird-women   175
Vito Apüshana
translated from the Spanish and Wayuu by Maurice Rodriguez

Grazing Land   179
Leonidas
translated from the Greek by Sherod Santos

Two Mapuche-Huilliche Poems   181
Jaime Huenún Villa
translated from the Spanish by Cynthia Steele

[Untitled]   185
Saeb Tabrizi
translated from the Persian by Kayvan Tahmasebian and
     Rebecca Ruth Gould

The mistress of the house   188
ko ko thett
translated from the Burmese by the author

The Reeling City   190
Najwa Bin Shatwan
translated from the Arabic by Mona Zaki

Contributor Biographies   197

Previous Publications   217

Notable Translations Published in 2022   219

In memory of Edith Grossman (1936–2023)

Coeditors' Introduction

Perhaps it begins with the way many people in the U.S. first learn a foreign language in school: as a matter of equivalences. Imagine what the vocabulary page in a German-language workbook might look like. On the left side: *Guten Tag. Wie geht's? Auf wiedersehen.* Arranged neatly in the right column, each item lined up with its equivalent on the left, are the English counterparts: *Hello. What's up? Goodbye.*

Given this introduction to other languages, one might be forgiven for thinking—as many people do—that translation is likewise quick and convenient, and that translators merely transform texts "word-for-word" from one language into another, matching words in one column with their faithful partners in another. But those of us who work between languages know that precise equivalences are limited and become ever rarer as the cultural or linguistic distance between the language pair widens. Single words are broken into constellations of potential meanings, and the translator must direct their telescope at the nearest one. Especially in literary writing, sense is only one part of what is at stake: the cadences of a writer's prose or the tightly wound skein of sound in their poetry—all of these are absolutely particular to their language and must be reconstructed by a translator in the raw materials of a different language. Translators also interpret imagery and ideas, elucidate foreign concepts and literary references, navigate cultural distance, and may even tease to the surface what was implicit or obscure in the original. Yet this work that translators do—equal parts creative and critical—often goes unnoticed. Too often, it goes unacknowledged. If it is discussed at all, it is only in terms of how well or poorly it serves the voice of the "original author."

One prominent example is classicist Emily Wilson's translation of the *Odyssey*, the first complete translation into English by a woman of Homer's foundational epic. Among Wilson's innovations are special attention paid to the subaltern in the text, such as the domestic women who are condemned to death for sleeping with Odysseus's suitors. She refused the terms used by previous translators, such as "whores," cleaving closely instead to the original Greek, writing simply, "these girls." For domestic workers genteelly called "servants" in previous translations, Wilson uses a more direct term: "slaves." In doing so, Wilson offers a re-reading of a text produced by a male-centered culture, troubles any ahistorical conception of ancient Greece as an egalitarian paradise, and draws attention to that society's heterogeneity. She also forces us to question our own values as inheritors of the text.

Thus, more than finding the "right" words, a translator must also consider the politics and ethics within and behind those words. Texts and the languages from which they originate do not exist in a void, but rather in a complex web of interrelationships shaped by geopolitical forces—the global circulation of capital, for instance, and the continued legacies of imperialism and colonialism. The contributions to this volume offer numerous excellent examples of this interrelation. Translators Edith Adams, Maurice Rodriguez, and Cynthia Steele each offer an experience of poetry originally conceived in both Spanish and Indigenous languages (Wayuu and Mapudungun). Israeli author Almog Behar reminds us that language "is not natural or neutral" and "is always political." This raises important, thorny questions: What is the translator's relationship to the source text? Of the source text to the receiving language? What is the power dynamic between the original text's author and the canon to which that author belongs—or does not belong?

Literary translators' work is not limited to the complex process of translation. They seek out authors and serve as their advocates in the U.S. publishing industry. In doing so, they serve as curators who help determine which texts are available for broader consumption in the United States and so must wrestle with the ethics of representation. Certainly they can efface signs of cultural or linguistic difference—the translation strategy of "domestication." But with a critical and imaginative leap, a translator can also rediscover or even subvert the sanctity of a "classic," helping us see it with new eyes. They can liken an unfamiliar genre to one that is known and loved. They can challenge the hegemony of the English language by producing works that maintain linguistic and syntactic distance. In these ways, a literary translation can draw attention to questions of power and conformity. It can highlight the frictions and inequalities between cultures. A literary translation can even choose *not* to establish those relationships of equivalence that many readers believe lie at the heart of our craft. The result can be a translation that is jarringly different from what the "original audience" might have read or defies established U.S. literary conventions or subverts earlier translations of a text. This anthology offers diverse examples of this: Samson Allal's translations of Hymn to Ra, Eirill Alvilde Falck's translations of thirteenth and fourteenth century Nordic runes, and Anita Gopalan's translation from Hindi of a short story.

This first edition of the anthology assembles writers from around the world, including some whose home communities and nations are engaged in violent conflict with one another. One poem selected by us (the four coeditors) and our guest editor for inclusion does not appear. The Ukrainian poet (who also cotranslated her work to English) withdrew her poem, because this collection includes work by a Russian writer. We are deeply sorry not to have "Such Love," the poem by Yuliya Musakovska, cotranslated to English by Olena Jennings and the poet, appear in this book.

Many of the public's assumptions about translation—its secondary and derivative nature, the mechanical and perfunctory process by which it is achieved—are also found in the institutions that should value literary translation the most: publishing houses. It is woefully common in the publishing industry for translators' names to be left off of book covers or out of royalty agreements. Literary translators are advocating for their art and profession, slowly shifting the cultural conversation. We honor the support of literary journals, including all of those cited in this volume, and a growing number of presses that celebrate translators' contributions and accomplishments.

In a widely circulated essay for *The Guardian*, published in September 2021, Jennifer Croft (translator of Nobel Laureate Olga Tokarczuk's *Flights*, among other stellar books) convincingly decries such frustrating and outdated practices: "[We] are the ones who control the way a story is told," she insists. "We're the people who create and maintain the translated book's style. Generally speaking we are also the most reliable advocates for our books, and we take better care of them than anybody else." Yes, yes, and yes.

With the reinstatement of the National Book Award for Translated Literature in 2018—thirty-five years after its discontinuation—and the new National Book Critics Circle Gregg Barrios Book in Translation Prize, the U.S. publishing industry appears freshly interested in the world and its literatures. Along with the surge in M.F.A. programs, literary journals, and presses offering literature in translation, there has been a marked rise of interest in the work of literary translators. Persuading U.S. presses to publish the work of foreign authors continues to be difficult—the statistic remains that only about 3 percent of the literary books published annually on the U.S. market are translations.

This anthology has two primary goals, as we build on this shift in how translation is conceived and discussed within the wider culture. First, it fills a gap within the U.S. publishing landscape as the first annual, multi-genre anthology that highlights the important artistic, cultural, and political work that translators do. As such, it creates an enduring platform for translation to be appreciated as an artform in its own right, not one to be discussed only in terms of its representational success or failure, but also in terms of the cultural stakes that play out in the realm of the 97 percent of books published in the U.S. each year that are *not* translations. Best Literary Translations also promotes the increasing number of U.S.-based journals—many of them from universities or small non-profits—that make international literatures available by broadening their audiences. We join in the efforts of those organizations that award and aid publication of translations and recognize translators by raising the status of their art. We are deeply grateful to each one of the fifty-two U.S. literary journals that nominated translations. Their work made this collection possible.

Second, Best Literary Translations strives to be a curative to parochial thinking. We present voices from around the world, paying special attention to lesser-known literatures and languages. The guiding vision of Best Literary Translations is to offer a counterpoint to the xenophobia and racism that have marked the last decade—and, truly, the entire history—of this country.

Critic Allison Grimaldi-Donohue writes in *Words Without Borders* (September 2021), "Translation is an inherently political undertaking, opening readers and writers to different versions of the world we share . . . [I]n a culture where we are now attempting to make space for less heard voices . . . we must also pay close attention to the works we translate . . . or else we risk repeating and reinscribing worn-out or mistaken cultural norms and limiting our visions of both literature and the future." The same is demanded of anthologists of translation as well. The five hundred submissions we (gratefully!) received for this inaugural edition included translations from sixty languages by authors from ninety-six different nations or autonomous regions. We are already looking forward to next year's submissions.

The composition of our editorial team reflects our political commitment: the three historically underrepresented world-language regions of Africa, the Middle East, and Asia each have their own designated editors, while translations from the Americas include not only dominant colonial languages such as Spanish, Portuguese, and French but also translations of work by Indigenous and First Nations writers. We four coeditors each reviewed all five hundred submissions for the anthology, discussing together the longlist that we passed on to our brilliant and devoted guest editor, Jane Hirshfield. (Please see that long list of finalists at the end of this volume. Our appreciation and congratulations to everyone—translators, authors, and journals—mentioned there!)

The resulting anthology that you now read comes from the work of many: we four coeditors and our guest editor, the editors of all the literary journals who combed through the translations they had published during 2022 and nominated their favorites, and the translators who created the nominated works. We developed the anthology entirely via video meetings and email messages, as we coeditors moved back and forth between nine countries on three continents. We offer our most effusive thanks to inaugural guest editor Jane Hirshfield, who was such a joy to work with in every way.

Best Literary Translations would not exist without the support of two other important figures in the U.S. literary community: Will Evans and Daniel Simon. *World Literature Today* Editor in Chief Daniel Simon provided endless good advice, patience, encouragement, and technical support as we launched this effort in 2020 and 2021. All this in addition to the beacon that *WLT* has been for translators and writers around the world for so many years. That long leadership is evidenced by the number of times *WLT*'s name appears in the bios of the authors and translators in this anthology—more than any other publication. Deep Vellum founder and publisher Will Evans also enthusiastically supported the project and gave it a home, for which we are forever grateful.

As we four coeditors read through the five hundred submissions of literatures from all over the world, we not only found translations that are great reads, worthy of our inaugural edition, but we also worked through questions regarding what makes a translation beautiful (or whether beauty is even a desirable trait) and the best representation of an original author's work as well as the language vehicle that comes with it. Alas, in spite of our best efforts, some languages and regions are still not nearly as well represented as we would have wished. It is our greatest hope that the example of this inaugural edition will stimulate more translation of literature from *all* regions of the world, and we hope to read them as we prepare future editions of this annual anthology.

Best Literary Translations exists thanks to the work of translators who tirelessly search for the most unique, engaging, and necessary literary voices from around the world—both those working today and those from other eras. Now we will let the quality and range of these selected works, the strong voices of both their original authors *and* their translators, speak for themselves.

Noh Anothai, Coeditor for Asian Literatures
Wendy Call, Coeditor for Literatures of the Americas
Öykü Tekten, Coeditor for Middle Eastern Literatures
Kọ́lá Túbọ̀sún, Coeditor for African Literatures

Guest Editor's Introduction

IN WORDS AND BEYOND THEM

Language and literature, made only of words, live both in words and beyond them. Sometimes between them. But also, always, in us: their human practitioners, beneficiaries, chorus, convocation, cocreators, progeny, and flock.

When I was seven or eight years old, I joined that congregation, going into a New York City stationery store on First Avenue between 20th and 21st Streets to scan the circular wire racks near the front door. I was there on my own, allowance money in hand, to select the first book I would buy for myself. I browsed, sampled, pondered—and brought home a Peter Pauper Press book of Japanese haiku. Now, over six decades later, it seems that I've followed the sounds and scents of that book for a lifetime.

Even for a child growing up in a housing project on the lower East Side of Manhattan, rain and moon, heat and shadow, are recognized as carrying meanings beyond the physical. Something allusive, elusive, awake, dappled, mysterious lived in those translated pages' weathers, frogs, and blossoms, something beyond their bringing news also of "elsewhere." They carried the sense that a surplus seeing and saying existed, that an altered, altering relationship to my own life and language might exist as well. And, too, the news that *elsewhere* and *here* were not separate, nor separate from me. A good poem, it's been said, expands the available stock of reality. Even more then, perhaps, a good translation. Reading in childhood the work of Bashō, Issa, and Buson,

I could not have understood their words' deeper dimensions. Yet through them I began to recognize the world as the Belfast-born poet Louis MacNeice described it: "incorrigibly plural."

My great good luck, as a reader and as a person, has been to have come of age in an era of blossoming translation. I've spent a lifetime reading works from languages I don't know: Greek tragedies, Nahuatl flower songs, erotic love poems written in second century Sanskrit. Kafka and Sappho, Hildegard of Bingen, Borges. Lady Murasaki, Primo Levi, and José Saramago, Su Tung Po and Marina Tsvetaeva. The *Eddas, Gilgamesh, The Dream of the Red Chamber, War and Peace.* The world's sacred texts and trickster tales, Sei Shōnagon's diary, Turgenev's sketches, the ghazals of Ghalib, Van Gogh's letters to his brother, anonymous song-lines mapping the interior of Australia. All given me by their translators' hours and years of close-work pondering, self-doubt, and questioning; by their middle of night, insomniac searching for a more accurate or more resinous word. This verb or that one? The definite or indefinite article, as one must be added in English? Should some extra information be offered to make clear a meaning that would have been understood by anyone alive in the place and time the work was written, or should that context, however indispensable, be left for a footnote? Is the original's tone sincere or might it be comic? How to translate, or not, the name of a bird that does not nest in the new language it's being brought into, of a fish never seen there, a dish not tasted?

And what of the music, the rhythms? A native Japanese speaker hears alternating patterns of five and seven syllables, whether in poetry or prose, as the sound of a different order of thinking and feeling. A speaker of American English hears rhyming iambic pentameter, the recurrences of litany or blues. The rhythms of a limerick are instantly recognized by an American-English reader as also an attitude and an intention. But an Urdu ghazal's repeated end-word may seem at first only baffling, the parallel tones of Chinese unconveyable, and the prosody of alternating five and seven syllables will go unnoticed.

The Saint Lucian poet Derek Walcott, in an essay on the self-translating Russian poet-in-exile Joseph Brodsky, speaks of "the desolations that accompany translation." Walcott describes the translator's cul de sac problem when the month-name "August" takes a masculine grammar in one language, while in another, the poet—in this case, Walcott himself—has personified August as "a housemaid-cook, her ebony head in a white kerchief as she whipped sheets from a clothesline in a house near the sea . . . "

Any writer who translates or is translated knows these problems. The pronoun "you" in English is gender-neutral and can turn toward any of seven or nine different meanings. In Polish, though, it must be male or female—making it simply impossible to translate, one translator told me, a poem of mine whose full effect depends on shifting from one meaning of "you" to another. And yet, a few years later, a different Polish translator included that poem in an anthology of American poets. I do not read Polish. I have no idea what Julia Hartwig's translation of my poem may seem to say, or how the poem's larger meaning is affected. Yet I am glad, on faith, that the poem has been brought into Polish.

There is the famous Italian saying, a cliché to evoke here: *Traduttore, traditore.* "Translator, traitor." For a person doing the translating (or in my case, cotranslating), the act seems, however humbling, at least possible. One tries, in bringing a thousand-year-old Japanese five-line *tanka* into English, to choose the grammatical voice and verb tense that most strengthen the poem. The original grammar often specifies neither; the receiving language requires them; you must choose.

Being translated, though, I've shaken my head at the complete implausibility of the task, when even within what seems a single language, confusions abound. In the U.S., pumpkin pie is the traditional closing sweet of the fall-harvest holiday dinner. In England, "pie" means a savory main dish, not a dessert (which is called, in the English of England, a "pudding"), and pumpkins are eaten only by livestock. A Japanese translator once asked, "By 'end,' did you mean 'finishing point,' 'goal,' or 'edge' like a board of wood has?" "All those, yes, you understand the meaning exactly." "Japanese doesn't do that." A Russian translator e-mailed that "long-legged" is a cultural stereotype for Americans, did I mean to imply that, and if not, might she say "spindly-legged" instead? "Does it sound good, musically?" I asked. "Very good," she replied, then moved on to whether the "foreign" in "foreign dust" should be of the invading barbarian kind or indicate only "from elsewhere."

And still, even knowing all this, when I read a work in translation, I take what is offered at its word. What else can a reader do? We choose a book, we start to read, and the pages include no crosshatch marks of the arduous choice-making, no smoke scent of sorrowful compromise, no crumpled sheets from the vertiginous liberty-takings slipped into the printed text. We take on faith that what we read is close to, or at least close enough to, the work's experiencing in the language of its creation.

In books where style is clearly foreground—Roberto Calasso's *The Marriage of Cadmus and Harmony* comes to mind, a triumph of singular brushwork in Tim Parks's translation, as does the poetry of Wislawa Szymborska, whose distinctive sensibility Clare Cavanagh and Stanislaw Baranczak's collaborative translations brilliantly carry—the reader can't help but hope their own experience is at least kin to that of readers of the Italian or Polish. And yet . . . I once began rereading *War and Peace* in the then-new translation by Richard Pevear and Larissa Volokhonsky but hadn't quite finished before leaving on a month-long trip. The book was heavy. I completed reading it in the only translation available at my destination: the Constance Garnett, published in 1904. Much was different—sentence rhythms, diction, even the characters' names—and still it was, after some read-justment, the same book.

I am, as by now must be evident, a forgiving reader of translated works. We all must be forgiving to read at all. The very act of turning ink shapes or pixels into meaning and world is a cognitively generous act, requiring of us every benefit of the doubt.

Translators are surely the harshest critics of one another's work, object-ing to one another's choices with continuous, demurring dismay. At scales large and small—as is broadly evident in the pages of this anthol-ogy—philosophies of translation can honorably widely differ. In "The Task of the Translator," the German critic Walter Benjamin propounds the preservation of difference—a sentence originally in German should, brought into English, retain an audible reminder of the original grammar and soundscape. (We might think of this as translation speak-ing as a living person does after changing places and languages: with an accent and syntax that hold their full background and history.) The Mexican poet Octavio Paz felt differently—he proposed that a trans-lator must try to evoke the same effects by different means. Robert Fitzgerald, whose translations from Greek gave me my first entrance into the tragedies, believed that what was not strange to a work's orig-inal readers should not seem odd to readers in the receiving language. Beauty should echo beauty, he felt—and his translation of the Roman poet Catullus's elegy for his brother remains, for me, among the most moving and beautiful translations ever made (and contains at least one invention of Fitzgerald's own). Libyan poet, editor, and translator Khaled Mattawa (who is among the translators included in this collec-tion) has in turn compared translation to playing a musical score—an act not of mechanical repetition, but of interpretation, bringing a work newly to life each time.

Some translators of poetry hew to the work's original forms, con-vinced that what was conceived in dactylic hexameter should remain there. Stephanie McCarter, a current classicist, chose to set her 2022 translation of Ovid's *Metamorphoses* into the iambic pentameter of blank verse, finding it the nearer equivalent. For an Anglophone, she writes, that meter "simply *sounds* like poetry, even to the untrained ear." Others choose hybrid or half-forms, slant rhymes, free verse. Visual conventions may come into poetry's translation also. In Western traditions, the jagged right margin tells you a poem is a poem, yet the translator-scholar Hiroaki Sato is adamant that haiku should be printed as a single line, not broken into three. In Japan, a poem's essential poemness is set by ear, not eye.

Any choice made in these realms, whether in poetry or in prose, risks losing something the writer would feel inextricable to the work; yet choices must still be made. For instance, how does one translate a pun, when even the use of homonyms has different resonance in different languages? In English, puns tend toward the comic; in other languages they are a neutral device for increasing meaning. (I know of only one that holds between languages: the word "pine" is used for trees and the emotion of longing in both English and Japanese.)

There's also the question of time. Some translations of older works deliberately keep the fragrance of antiquity in them—the King James Bible, for instance, was famously brought by its committee of translators into a style and diction of English already a little archaic, to instill in its words the authority of a sacred text long in place. In her illuminating translator's preface to the *Metamorphoses*, Stephanie Carter advises not antique diction, but the practice of a stringent temporal hygiene. When later cultural attitudes and habits of mind are brought into earlier texts, she writes, those intrusions shift not only qualities of surface, but the work's fundamental worldview and world. Other translators are blatantly and unapologetically anachronistic. This collection includes an Eleventh-Dynasty Egyptian hymn whose singer, four thousand years ago, surely knew nothing of origami, microchips, or bulletproof vests.

Most often, translated works are brought into a more quietly contemporary diction and current aesthetic. This transmigration can make older pieces available in new ways. I was once asked to present *The Ink Dark Moon*, my cotranslation of the work of the two foremost Japanese women poets of the Heian era, to a graduate class at a Tokyo university. Ono no Komachi wrote in the ninth century, Izumi Shikibu at the turn of the millennium. I'd thought the request odd—would a group of students in Boston want to hear Emily Dickinson in Japanese? I was mistaken. The students said they were hearing the poems for the first time as relevant to their own lives, as genuinely moving—a response I attribute more to the erasing of a thousand years of dust than to the specifics of Mariko Aratani's and my choice of words. Poems brought into current-day English could speak as they did when first written: as this moment's murmur into this moment's ear.

Only a few of the pieces included in this anthology are from earlier eras. I found it interesting that, at least of the finalist group I received, the prose translations were all of works more or less contemporary, while poetry translators continue to bring forward voices from the deep and recent past as well as the present. I must guess that some earlier works of prose unknown to English-language readers still wait to be found—and with them, perhaps, some increased stocks of available reality as indispensable to humanity's long-term resilience as the native plant seeds now being stored in the Svalbard Global Seed Vault.

In his five Massey Lectures delivered for the CBC in 2022, the Indigenous Canadian writer, playwright, and musician Tomson Highway spoke of the different selves his three different languages evoke. English, as he experiences himself in speaking it, is a language "above the neck," good for matters of mind. French he finds the language of heart and stomach. His birth-language, Cree, he describes as sexual, scatalogical, and immutably funny—onomatopoetic, quickening, a language that laughs at and along with existence.

Languages, then, have their own sensibilities, and these qualities, too, a translation must try to convey, bending the receiving language beyond its home-ground capacities, opening tongue and ear to alternative ways of being, hearing, knowing, feeling. By this process of exchanging capacities, news, gossip, worldviews, and knowledge, cultures broaden, become more capacious. This, too, is the gift of the translations found in this volume. They hold specific experiences, yes, to be tasted and walked inside of, but carry also translation's fundamental increase of perspective, perception, and possibility, of what can be said, and how.

I will not attempt to describe here the full range of what these pages hold—readers can turn the pages and see for themselves. Their writers come from Eritrea, Chile, Iran, Korea, Norway, Poland, Kurdistan, India, the island of La Réunion. Past, present, and future in turn find their recordings, envisionings, and imagining. A sea krait titles one piece, a lion another. One selection here was assembled from the words of a group of gathered ex-combatants from a conflict zone. Another is missing, withdrawn by its author for reasons of conscience, as described elsewhere. Its absence, though the decision must be respected, grieves me. The larger causes for its absence raise a grief far greater.

The works reprinted in these pages emerged from a set of finalists first winnowed by this series' remarkable, infinitely curious, passionately engaged and warmly collegial team of four permanent editors, pulled from five hundred journal-published pieces nominated in response to a general call. Before that, they had been winnowed from the broader pool of translations read by the editors of the literary journals in which the works first appeared. Before that came the winnowing done by the translators themselves, who selected these particular pieces to bring into English, devoting to them their time, attention, talents, tongues. Before that, the winnowing done by the original writers—these are the words chosen from previous drafts, from pages never shown to others, from all the possible stories, poems, sentences, observations that might have been written.

Somewhere, in a Borgesian infinite library or the branching universes posited by certain physicists, are innumerable works missing here and from all other visible shelves. For all that is omitted, I offer the trust of future finding.

When asked to judge any competition or award process, I'm powerfully aware how arbitrary the end result will necessarily be. No two judges would arrive at a set of identical choices. This is, of course, why the practice of rotating the final guest editor each year is so useful— one year's tilt will be balanced by the next. Still, I came to this task with the intention of not choosing solely by personal preference. I was asked from the start to select as broadly representative a group of works as possible, especially given that this is the inaugural volume of a series whose aspirations include an increased awareness of work being done by writers worldwide. Luckily, just such a range arrived in my own set of finalist choices without any extra weighting or effort— works drawn from many languages, aesthetics, subjects, sources, and styles of translation rose to the top on their own. I was also aware, in my own weighing, that this is not an anthology recognizing only the qualities of the original works, though that of course could hardly be set aside. This anthology series exists to recognize specifically the work, gifts, and strengths of *translators*, those who give Anglophones access to the writing—and lives—of the beyond-English-speaking world.

In the most fundamental dimension, I made my selections in a state of ignorance—almost all the included pieces come from languages I cannot read. I relied on those who came before me in the process for that realm of evaluation. I could only judge the English-language version, the piece that arrived on the page, and that is, perforce, what I did. One more paradox of the process here comes to mind: in some cases—not all—a translator's wish is to become, to be found, virtually transparent. Yet here we hope to notice, admire, and honor that impossible feat.

It's said that the world loses a language every two weeks. With that language, a unique ecosystem of knowledge and history vanishes also. As with the disappearing animals and plants, we race against quickening extinction. Each work in this book is a small act of both preservation and cross-pollination—each writer's vision, sensibility, and concerns are, as the word "translation" holds at its root, carried across. In those moments of carrying, a conjoining occurs. Both receiver and text live afterward changed; some new hybrid of experience, language, and understanding comes into being. The act of translating, especially, asks of a person a willing vulnerability and agreed-to exposure, a dropping away of the boundaried defenses of a fixed self. The act of translating opens the psyche's innermost rooms to the unknown. Free of preconceptions and opinion, you must know what is there on its own terms before you can judge it. This is the opposite of this moment's barraging news, inside the U.S., of acts of stand-your-ground deadly violence and the deliberately fanned fear of the "other" that lies behind it. A translator is a person offering home ground and welcome to others, as is also a reader, first starting a book. This simple, basic widening of self, psyche, and sense of community—to curiosity; to the magnets of beauty, story, laughter; to the tastes and shapes of the new; to the embrace of questioning, embrace of feeling, embrace of eros over thanatos and mutuality over power—this is one counterweight to the fear, self-assertion, tribalism, and division of our current socio-political era.

Translation, then, and our continuing practice and support of it, has—as the four series-editors have said so eloquently in their own introduction—a transformative social dimension. Welcoming the sheer variousness and plurality of all lives; holding the desire to feel what others have felt, to see what they have seen, to imagine what they have imagined; wanting to know oneself not as soloist but as part of a larger chorus and wanting that full chorus heard, its full music sung across time, place, culture, language, causes and conditions—this is the path of kinship rather than closure. To write, translate, read the stories and poems of our lived interconnection is to be part of the work of *tikkun olam*, the repair of the world—needed now, needed always. Yet we need not feel this as weight or obligation. It is simply what happens when a person is curious enough to pick up a book about things they don't already think, holding lives they don't already know.

I commend to you this first annual anthology of Best Literary Translations. It honors those whose shadow work, too often unnoticed and essential, makes possible a wider, wilder, more varied, generous, and multi-dimensional knowing of who we are on this earth, together. It has been my great pleasure and gladness to have been a small part of its coming into your hands.

Jane Hirshfield

May 1, 2023
Mill Valley, California
Mount Tamalpais Arroyo Corte Madera del Presidio Watershed
on the unceded land of the Coastal Miwok people

Near the Shrine of Saint Naum

Najwan Darwish
translated from the Arabic by Kareem James Abu-Zeid
Words Without Borders

I stood in the red church,
its tiny domes like buds
blossoming in stone,
I stood near the saint's resting place
while a tourist laid her cheek on the tombstone
to hear his beating heart.
But I was no tourist,
and the saint left the room with me,
and the church the builders wrote in his memory
was nothing more
than a passing dream in his eternal sleep.

The tourists come in vain,
as do the believers.

Translator's Note

This poem is about a specific place and a specific moment in time. I've been translating Najwan Darwish's work for over a decade now, and I work very closely with him, as his English is superb. Concerning the story behind this poem, Darwish did not offer any specific information, and he often resists providing explanations or interpretations of his texts, preferring to let the poetry speak for itself. But I do know that Darwish has traveled to Macedonia, and that he always writes from his own life experience. So there is no doubt in my mind that this poem emerged from time actually spent at the shrine in question.

Saint Naum's monastery is located on the shores of Lake Ohrid in the southwestern corner of present-day Northern Macedonia, just a stone's throw from the Albanian border. Naum was born sometime around 830 or 835 CE, in what was then the First Bulgarian Empire, and was as much a literary figure as a religious one. He was a disciple of the Byzantine theologians Cyril and Methodius, two brothers who—along with Naum and other disciples—were credited with inventing both the Glagolitic and Cyrillic alphabets. Naum was also one of the founders of the Pliska Literary School, and an active member of the Ohrid Literary School. I would encourage readers to delve more deeply into the life of this fascinating figure, the literary schools he was involved in, and the cults that emerged around him after his death.

Najwan Darwish frequently notes that he is a spiritual man, but not a religious one, so I imagine that what first drew this contemporary Palestinian poet to the shrine was not Naum's religious or missionary work, but rather the more spiritual aspects of Naum's life, coupled with the saint's prolific literary activities.

From *Guerrilla Blooms*

Daniela Catrileo
translated from the Spanish by Edith Adams
New England Review

It's hard to say:
is this a tapir
or
is this fear

I can't decide
if the image existed
in this universe
of things

Because
tapir and fear
lay outstretched
in repose
to the eclipse prior
to their words

Just as I   was also myself
before the creation of this poem

We carry traces of blood stamped
upon gold and brown skin

A painting that sketches
          the map of the stars

—that is our language—

Not a word that imitates
          but a figure that's traced

A frenzy of vultures waits till we fall

How many sisters have fallen
already?

I look toward the hills:
black clouds and plantations

We don't have a marching band
but once it rained fish
I ask myself what would've happened
if they
had never
arrived

They?
He?

Which
word
to name

Which
land
to maim

I don't know if we are
catastrophe
or the dream of the absent
bird

Translator's Note

These excerpts were originally published in *New England Review* 43.4 and come from a larger project currently titled *Guerrilla Blooms*, the Spanish/Mapudungun-to-English translation of Daniela Catrileo's 2018 poetry collection *Guerra florida/Rayülechi malon*. In recent years, Daniela Catrileo has become an essential voice in both Chilean letters and Mapuche cultural production. Her poetics reflects on the contours and multiplicities of Mapuche identity in the wake of exile, migration, and colonization, both historical and ongoing.

Originally appearing in print as a bilingual Spanish-Mapudungun edition, *Guerrilla Blooms* reimagines the arrival of the colonizers from the perspective of an Indigenous woman who, alongside her partner and a collective of other women warriors, takes up arms against them. Comprised of individual poems connected by an overarching narrative, the text is a work of poetic fiction that explores the crossing of multiple territories, languages, and Indigenous imaginaries and subverts the dominant narrative of colonization told from the perspective of the invaders.

These particular excerpts thematize problems of language and naming that continue well after the formal end to colonial rule. In the same way that Daniela asks, "Which word to name," there are many names quietly sharing the space of my own as this text's translator; indeed, translation by its very nature is rarely, if ever, a solitary practice. These translations have emerged from invaluable feedback offered in translation workshops at USC, Bread Loaf, and the *Kenyon Review*; from classmates and colleagues who graciously offered feedback and edits; and from Daniela herself, with whom I have exchanged hundreds of messages over the past few years related to this project. Her willingness to help me understand difficult passages and her trust in me to make this something new in English have been essential to the creation of these poems.

Hymn to Ra

unknown author
translated from the Old Egyptian by Samson Allal
Poetry

*From the tomb stela of King Wahankh Intef II, pharaoh of the Eleventh Dynasty
of Egypt, 2108–2059 BCE*

Accept me, Ra, before you go,
before I go,
I pray . . .

Do polychromatic dawn threads
coat you,
like the tiny coruscating disks
sewn into a sequin dress?

Bring me to the breast of the night,
let me suckle stars,
cuddle obsidian cosmos ancestors . . .

They honor you, Ra,
like I do.
We sing your praises when you rise,
we weep
whenever you duck under the earth.

Embrace me, like a mother, O eternal night!
Fold me,
like a black origami flamingo,
forever protected
by dark paper, dark praise . . .

Let all be run by your rule, Ra!

You know I'm your right-hand man, right?

You made me into a microchip,
a code that doesn't die . . .

Hand me over to the hours
of day and night.
Time is my bulletproof vest.

I'm an ankle-tagged newborn
tongue-tied to the nipple of dawn,
the teat of dusk.

A child of the dark,
midnight skies move over my skin,
black-limbed angels of unburdened air,
ardent guardians,
keep me close,
but I fear the bulls with backward horns . . .

O hula hoop of light, eye of Ra,
unremitting rage,
you are my 24/7 security squad,
discover me as your gift . . .

Translator's Note

According to the Metropolitan Museum of Art, which holds the original stela (the stone slab inscribed with the hieroglyphs which make up the original Hymn to Ra), the poem was found in the tomb of King Intef II Wahankh, third Pharaoh of the eleventh dynasty, a period of political disorder in Egypt. This disorder and desire for unity is reflected in the original message of the text. Intef II stood out to me, as did his Hymn, or the Hymn ascribed to him, because there is a combination of grandeur and humility . . . a tenderness, a Fertile Crescent. Intef II seemed to express the scope of human fears. Fears of the unknown. Human longings for belonging, for unity with nature, with life, for the settling of scores, for eternal tranquility.

In terms of the actual composition of the poem, terms like re-creation or transformation may be more accurate than translation, unless we are looking at the word translation the way ancient poets understood the role of the poet—as the interpreter, the messenger, the sage, the conduit of a spirit, a language, a muse. The word translate comes from the Latin "transferre," to carry across. The poet is always a carrier, a carrier of experience, a translator of experience. A poem is an event, an event in time, and like any event its existence is in its record, its echo. So, returning to the Hymn to Ra, it is this visual echo, an assemblage of signs, the symbols on the stela, the basic, literal translations available, but moreover the overall inspiration for the translation was the concept, the belief, ultimately, in an ultimate sun, an absolute father, and a motherly unknown beyond the known world, a tender abyss, or a loving oblivion.

We Will Survive

Rolla Barraq
translated from the Arabic
    by Muntather Alsawad and Jeffrey Clapp
MAYDAY

Death was passing through the pores of waiting
like fresh messages from the sky:
We will survive!
The rain will return, sweet and drinkable, in September.
The children will go to school.
They will read "Home" or "The boy planted a rose" or "The girl
    fed a cat."
They will draw houses with large open doors and no fences.
Teenage boys will agree to play a soccer match or bet on a game
    of billiards.
A girl will smile because she has become taller with prettier eyes.
A shy young man will decide to tell the girl he liked for three
    years that she is
        sweeter than the moment of salvation.
And the girl who forgot her bag on the bus . . . she will untie her
    braid in front of the mirror.
The father will hug his children when he comes home from work.
The mother will read them interesting stories before bed.
And the grandma who is always angry . . . she will sing all day
    long.
The grocery salesman will get louder
        and fear will creep out of the city.

We would have survived
    if the war hadn't swallowed the alleys up, one by one,
    and thrown their ruins into us!

Translators' Note

We met when Jeff was a volunteer tutor at Learning Works in Portland and Muntather was a young man from Basra looking to improve his English skills. When we discovered our mutual passion for literature, however, we quickly abandoned those roles for the pursuit of poetry. Along with his own poems, Muntather brought in older Iraqi verses he had begun to translate into English. After collaborating on several of these, Jeff suggested they turn to untranslated work by living Iraqi poets. Muntather used his contacts back home to uncover a string of over thirty interesting poets from different parts of the country. Rolla Barraq was one, a young woman from Mosul, a city that had been hit particularly hard by ISIS-fueled violence.

She was a reliable source, easy to communicate with and forthcoming with a series of poignant poems that have resonated with an American audience. "We Will Survive" is one of these, a poem that draws on the recurrent themes of social upheaval and unending war that have plagued Iraq since the 1980s. Nonetheless, there is more sunlight in Rolla's verse than most of her male peers, a hopefulness that may derive in part from a woman's focus on the next generation.

Our process has remained roughly the same throughout: Muntather chooses the poet and the poem and makes a first draft in English. He sends it to Jeff, who continues the work of turning those words into a faithful but effective English language poem. We then confer in person, going back and forth over issues of literal and cultural meaning, word choice, line breaks—everything—until we are satisfied with the outcome. It is then Jeff's job to send the poem into the world. In this way, we have forged a very equal and effective partnership.

Neighbor

Yoo Heekyung
translated from the Korean by Stine Su Yon An
The Southern Review

The tree branches in the empty lot congealing into thickness—it
    was that kind of summer
Or maybe it was winter—such details are unimportant
With something akin to determination, I remember my neighbor
    standing under the blazing sun like a hardened piece of
    bread
He had moved in with just a single emaciated clothes hanger
The sun that day stooped down at a peculiar angle, and he was
    trembling, a little, like a sloughed off overcoat

I pound on the iron doors of his house, sturdy as teeth, and
    make a request *Who is it?* I am your next-door neighbor,
    could I perhaps borrow a candle? *There is nothing here* He
    has no further words for me through the doorknob He
    stands in the dark and merely stares at the pallid door

Since the day he moved in I've grown thinner and thinner
On some early mornings, I hear an extended whistling from his
    house I wake from my sleep, and with my neighbor's pet
    in mind, I curl up smaller and smaller into the awkward
    blankets On those days, endless shadows fill my dreams,
    trembling little by little

He discarded the clothes hanger in a corner of the empty lot and
    moved away
I remember the appearance of him leaving as something akin to
    a misunderstanding
From time to time, I stand there like the wrapper freshly torn
    from the cigarette pack, and while hanging a shadow on the
    clothes hanger, I think—why is it that neighbors are such
    loose things, such dark and narrow hallways
Like the shadow sagging on the clothes hanger, I tremble slowly
    slowly

Translator's Note

I was introduced to Yoo's work through the poet and translator Don Mee Choi. She mentioned that Yoo had studied poetry with the poet Kim Hyesoon, ran a poetry bookshop, and was active as a playwright in Seoul. I was intrigued by Yoo's poetic lineage and impact as a cultural worker and writer.

In 2020, I had the chance to work on translations of Yoo's poems through the Emerging Translator Mentorship Program from ALTA. I chose to translate poems from Yoo's first collection, *Oneul achim daneo* (Moonji Books, 2011), because as an emerging poet, I was interested in Yoo's earlier work from his time as an emerging writer. His debut collection introduces his poetics and the vocabulary he builds and refines in his later poetry and essay collections. "Neighbor" is one such poem and vocabulary entry. In *Today's Morning Vocabulary* (my working title for the translated collection), Yoo presents lyrical, lineated poems and prose poems that chronicle contemporary life in a minor key. In translating Yoo's work, I find that his poems often provide the reader with both the rain and the umbrella for the rain. This is a world where even sadness finds that it too has its own silvery sparkle. It's an immense pleasure and honor to introduce new readers to Yoo's poetry.

Family Portrait of the Black Earth

Yordanka Beleva
translated from the Bulgarian by Izidora Angel
Firmament

After the surgeons removed my grandmother's breast, she began to cup her hands over the bare spot. The way you'd hide a physical discomfort. Baba's cupped hand, which I'd known both as a den of endearment and as a unit of time, was now also the dome of a church. A demolished church. We stood before the ruins and made out the details in the frescoes: the doctors' late diagnosis, our belated prayers.

The village women came by to visit and check on her, see how she was feeling. Pain and suffering are strange tourist attractions. In some places around the world, large-scale tragedies have their price of admission: houses where for years someone got held and tortured, schools where mass shootings took place, stretches of road along-side train wreckages. Baba's wound was free and open to the public. Sometimes she'd tell her visiting girlfriends that the only thing that hurt was her missing breast but none of them could wrap their heads around how a piece of flesh long severed from the body could hurt.

A few times Baba sent my grandfather over to the hospital to retrieve her breast so they could bury it in the garden. It was a good garden; it had yielded good harvests for years. But this wasn't an organ to be planted, the only thing it was good for was a lab culture.

Dyado pretended he'd gone to see the doctors as my grandmother had asked him. Once, he came back and lied that they wouldn't release the breast without special paperwork. Other times he claimed they'd missed some sort of deadline. But he could only beat around the bush for so long. And one day, he came home with something from the butcher. He unwrapped it and pounded this delicacy methodically, therapeutically, until he became rawer than the raw meat. But the therapy hadn't worked. For someone on the outside looking in, Dyado must have looked like a diligent farmer prepping his winter provisions. Curing sausage, for instance, was also best done over the smoke of a smoldering fire. Dyado kept the meat away from the cats and from Baba until it shriveled enough to resemble the corpse of a breast.

Baba and Dyado dug a shallow hole close to the grave of Karaman, the dog. Afterward, they interred the breast corpse and covered the hole. They did not stand on ceremony. For my grandmother it was important that she be reunited with all her body parts; she believed she could not leave the earthly realm had a part of her body been mislaid. For my grandfather, it was important to fulfill her final wish to be whole.

She outlived her breast by eight years.

We covered a lot of ground during that time. We attempted to act as though nothing had happened. It's what you might call conversational camouflage. Even so, the disguise dematerialized every time: a sudden question on whether I recalled the name of that one song about the severed head of the partisan fighter Vela Peeva; what if Dyado had brought her another woman's breast by mistake and that woman was now desperately searching for it somewhere; for the millionth time, to look closely at her—see how on the left side, her body was that of a young girl and on the right, that of a decrepit old woman. Our conversations took on that same asymmetry: to the left, an echo; to the right, a silence.

She never visited the breast burial site and like all neglected graves, this one too quickly weeded over. Once, Baba told me how she'd diligently tended to her garden her entire life—she weeded from dawn till dusk because weeds were like cancer, they swiftly stifled the good plants and suffocated them. She ought to have tended to her health as she'd tended to her garden, she said. Be a good gardener, she told me.

I wonder sometimes whether keeping silent on what we'd really buried in the garden was the right thing to do. I saw something on the news once about two cousins who'd tried to rig the lottery by leaving their number picks off the original ticket and waiting to write in the winning numbers on their carbon copy only after they'd seen the results called on TV. They'd forgotten that the winning ticket could only be authenticated by matching all the tear-offs to the original. Dyado was a good criminal, I thought, he had switched out Baba's torn-off piece so well, she felt like a winner even in her biggest loss. But that's not to say this is a hopeful story.

I'm not fond of hopeful platitudes, especially ones about cups that are half-full. Maybe it's because I've seen what an empty brassiere looks like.

At home, empty bras are archaeological finds from a long ago dried up Milky Way. Elsewhere, they are testimonials to the soft landing of motherhood, flags signaling the capitulation of childhood. All empty brassieres are unhappy: something has left, somebody has followed. We've yet to invent replacement padding to even out the heart's losses and keep them artificially half-full.

A strange plant is shooting up from the ground near where we buried the rotted meat. If I like it, I'll call it Baba's lullaby.

Translator's Note

Even an 880-word micro story like "Family Portrait of the Black Earth" has a long journey because art takes a long time to gestate and travel and Bulgarian words famously take a long time to get their passports.

It was instantly clear to me that Yordanka Beleva was a bewitching writer and a master of the short form. Meeting her in person was just as bewitching; she's the real thing. Her folkloric yet contemporary, woman-centric style is at turns sensual and devastating, political without being preachy, godly without being sermonic. Like the story included here, most stories in *Keder* take place in a village and they concern women's relationship to pain and grief and other women and sometimes men.

I wanted to be gentle with the hallowed imagery at the top of the story so as not to overwhelm the aesthetic. I kept *baba* (grandma) and *dyado* (grandpa) throughout the collection because I didn't want to disappear the Bulgarian—which inevitably also means sometimes keeping the Turkish, like *keder* (sorrow), for instance. I also felt strongly that I needed to keep some of the melody of the original Bulgarian, which can be heard in a sentence like this one: "Baba and Dyado dug a shallow hole close to the grave of Karaman, the dog."

Story collections in translation are famously difficult to publish, but I couldn't keep from trying. I was thrilled to be at Bread Loaf to work on this with none other than Jenny Croft and I was just as thrilled to work on it with the brilliant writers in my Chicago translators' collective, Third Coast Translators Collective. Before the NEA grant and being included in anthologies such as this one, it was the journals and their editors, like Jessica Sequeira at *Firmament*, who gave the stories a chance. Thank you. It takes a village, truly.

00572

Julia Rendón Abrahamson
translated from the Spanish by Madeleine Arenivar
Another Chicago Magazine

Ivan comes out of the bathroom shirtless. He's skinny, with just a few hairs that, strangely, trace a straight line from the middle of his chest down to his navel. Catalina is lying on the bed, face up and naked. When she hears him coming, she turns over. She sticks out her ass, arching her lower back so it looks bigger, and opens her legs a little. Ivan slaps her on one of her butt cheeks and tells her she's delicious, then he bends down to look for his button-down shirt and white coat under the bed. Before he puts them on, he goes over to the plain pine desk and chugs one of the bottles of water standing there. He's sure Catalina refills them because the water always tastes like tap. He's very thirsty, and while he drinks, he looks out the window with its white plastic frame, covered by transparent curtains. This neighborhood of Quito has always seemed dirty to him, teeming with people. He remembers how, when he was a kid, his dad always bought his doctor's cases in a leather goods store nearby. He always went with him, gritting his teeth, until he turned eighteen. On the cusp of entering medical school, he finally had the courage to tell him that he didn't want to go anymore. He doesn't understand what people see in these old colonial buildings and houses; he thinks they're hideous, unlivable, with those tiny windows, all dark and outdated.

Catalina gets up and goes over to him. She takes the bottle from his lips and drinks from it. Her hair is long and dyed blonde, and her mouth is still red from the lipstick that she bought from a friend who works for Yanbal, who promised her it wouldn't come off for anything. Ivan puts on his shirt and Catalina, finished with the water, buttons it for him. Ivan's hand rests close to her thigh and, knowing, she moves closer to graze against it. While she's buttoning she keeps moving, so his hand touches her thigh, then her pussy, grazing, grazing. Ivan grabs her from behind, fiercely, not her ass but her legs. His hands sink in, dwarfed by Catalina's colossal thighs. She finishes buttoning his shirt and he squeezes her and growls that he has to go back to the clinic. She disentangles herself, walks away and flops down on the bed.

"According to my calendar, tomorrow or the day after you get your period, right? I want to start the tests next week."

"But you promised me that first I could go see Maca." As she speaks, she opens and closes her legs, touches her hair.

"I already told you, you have to rest."

Catalina stops shifting her legs, she keeps them together and covers herself with the sheet. Above it, she touches her flat stomach. What else can she say? She thinks that it will be over a year since she's seen her daughter. She thinks about Bogotá, about her friends, how good it would feel to be back. When Ivan comes over to give her a kiss she stands up and puts her t-shirt on, hot pink, with a cartoon of an ice cream with a cherry on top. It's tight over her chest. She can't find her underwear, and when she stands up to look for it, Ivan takes the opportunity to smack her on the ass again as he leaves, saying that the secretary will send her the details for her admission later.

Catalina has never had problems giving birth. Even with Maca, her first, at just sixteen years old, she was only in labor for an hour. She almost didn't make it to the aunt's house who helped her push. She didn't go to a hospital—with the traffic in Bogotá, she's sure she would have ended up giving birth in a taxi! Maca was born with her eyes wide open and she never cried. She had a lot of hair, very black. As soon as she came out, Catalina herself caught her with both hands; she was slippery with that white stuff all over her body. Now

she knows it's called vernix. Ivan explained it to her. Maca was so tiny.
When she looked down and realized she was still bleeding she handed
her to the aunt, and she remembers clearly how she asked if her stom-
ach would stay so floppy. Her aunt whisked the baby away and said
that she would bring her back in a bit to breastfeed. Maca just watched
with those big eyes, she still didn't cry. Now that she thinks about it,
her daughter has never cried much. Not even when she went out to
party and left her with her aunt, not when Maca's father hit her, not
caring whether the little girl was watching, not when she started day-
care or kindergarten, nothing. And even less when they said goodbye
and Catalina promised her she would come back soon. She wonders if
she cries when she's alone. She feels like talking to Maca, but when she
calls the phone rings and no one answers. Anyhow, she realizes that at
this hour she must be in school.

No other child of hers—more like, no other baby—has come out
with their eyes wide open like Maca's. She's named them all, but she
hasn't told and will never tell Ivan. She knows he would be angry. He
always says that if she gets attached, she'll fuck it up; he's even threat-
ened to not pay her if she gets fond of one of the babies. He's explained
the plan to her a thousand times. He's told her a thousand times which
tests are mandatory, what exercises she has to do, what she has to say,
where she has to give birth, who she shouldn't talk to, what to answer
to each question, what photos she should take, where she should go.
He's also told her that if the mom says she should walk, she walks,
if the mom wants her to eat only red meat, she'll eat a whole cow, if
the mom wants her to be a vegetarian, she'll eat lettuce and that's it.
Plus, his office sends her food for all nine blessed months. Anyhow,
these moms now, they're just a pain in the ass, they don't want you
to have even one ice cream or drink a Coke. So fucking lame! When
she was pregnant with Maca she even smoked a little weed and noth-
ing bad happened. Yeah, and don't even think about smoking ciga-
rettes. Ivan really threatened her over that. One time he told her that if

she smoked, he would go himself directly to the Ministry and demand that they take away her refugee visa. After how hard she worked to get that stupid visa. She still gets the dry heaves when she remembers the rusty smell of the dick of the old man in Immigration who had to sign the last form she needed. Down in the big office in Quitumbe, in that disgusting back bathroom.

In any case, she does give them names. How would Ivan find out? The only thing missing is for him to put cameras in her apartment. Plus, how could she not give them names? Talk to someone for nine months without calling them something. What else could she call them, boy 1, girl 2, girl 3? She wants to keep going, but Ivan has told her this is the last one, that she's not so young anymore. He thinks she probably can't take another liposuction. Ivan likes her to be totally flat after.

She goes over to the window and drinks from the bottle of water that's left. She looks out and sees a girl about three years old playing with a deflated ball. Her face is dirty and there's a rip in her t-shirt. Cata looks for the mother in the corner store or on the sidewalks nearby, but she doesn't spot her. The girl runs from one side to the other, veering around the people walking by. Cata realizes her legs are cold. She turns around to look for her jeans. She looks at the old clock hanging over the bed. It's not one yet. She wants to wait a bit before calling again. Maybe she can go down and get something to eat.

Her other children—the boys and girls, whatever—she didn't catch them, of course. She never felt if they were slippery, but she can imagine it. They're all born with that white stuff, but in the hospitals, who knows why, they're determined to wash them as soon as possible. She remembers how delicious Maca's skin was, how warm she was. How nervous she was that she would slip out of her hands. She was just a little sixteen-year-old baby, she never imagined she would have more kids.

What will this new chick want, girl or boy? Who knows, but they all ask for a natural birth. It would be easier to have a C-section with anesthesia, wouldn't it? The last old lady wanted to walk together every day in the Parque Metropolitano. That was Gael's mom, although she thinks that later they called him Eduardo. At least, that's what his mom called him after the walks. Cata realized that the lady was kind of embarrassed to talk to her belly, to touch her, but she did it anyways. She blushed, but she did it. It was her son in the end, no? Catalina always thought that Eduardo sounded like a name for an old man. A person who's born already old. This one, definitely, felt like a Gael.

Catalina decides not to go down. She dials her daughter's phone number again.

Translator's Note

I first met Julia Rendón Abrahamson through the kind of serendipi-
tous social connection that leads to the saying "Quito es un pueblo."
The fact that we were connected through a chain of mothers' chat
groups seems fitting, considering that her work centers themes of gen-
der, family, and class—and particularly the roles of women. Her realist
stories shine a light on the weak points, the hypocrisies and uncom-
fortable parallels that exist everywhere in twenty-first century urban
Latin America. With spare, graceful language, she draws back the cur-
tain on families and their silences, and on the ways that relationships
of power permeate seemingly private interactions. "00572" is one
of my favorite stories from her collection *Yeguas y terneros* (2021)
because of the masterful way in which a single short scene unfolds
into a complex web of power calling into question larger political real-
ities that make up the cities we live in every day—parallel stories we
never see. Rendón Abrahamson's writing makes us stop and look at
the work women do—by choice, by coercion, or by default—making
visible what is too often hidden.

Graceless

Samwai Lam
translated from the Chinese by Natascha Bruce
The Massachusetts Review

He presses against me and for a moment I feel the weight of him. It's something real, then it's gone.

My Lord.

His movements stop and his eyes widen. He stares at me in alarm, as if he's suddenly realized I'm his best friend, or his ex, or maybe his daughter. Panic dilates his pupils and I am flooded with compassion.

He looks scared, like a newborn baby the moment it opens its eyes and encounters the world for the first time. I reach for him. I have an urge to stroke his cheek, to bring him hope. My palm presses against his face. His skin is rough and his breath smells of meat. His hand is on my stomach, the palm calloused. With his back to the light, his features are obscured and rays emanate from his body, like an image of God.

That's why I say: My Lord.

He pulls away from me and rushes out of the room. To ask the shopkeeper his results, to subject himself to the scrutiny of the shopkeeper's artificial eye. He won't dare express doubts in the presence of that eye; he'll confess them later, to his Google search bar.

The shopkeeper's eye will roll back in his head, scanning the man's data.

According to the wrist monitor on my left arm, my mental and physical performances have been good. Five stars on all counts. My oxygen saturation level was satisfactory and, most importantly, my memory did not glitch. My tears, expressions, and reactions were all exactly in line with the man's advance requests.

Storming out to consult with the shopkeeper could also have been an advance request. Some people like to see themselves as the injured party. Between those who inflict harm and those who receive it, the receiver is always the more easily satisfied.

My wrist monitor shows full marks, a perfect score. I'm not surprised.

In here, they call me God.

The door closes, and all my attention is on them. I let them do whatever they want, make all their desires come true.

When I have to work, it's daytime. When I don't have to work, it's night.

My eyes open, the light is bright white, and my wrist monitor tells me there's already someone outside the door, waiting. The room next to mine, as always, is quiet. Outside my door, I hear shuffling foot-steps and nervous breathing. They're entering the presence of God; of course they're afraid. Afraid, humbled, awed. And then they step in here, into this blankness, this room with only a bed, and the dynamic flips. Then I am in complete service to their every desire.

There's nothing sharp in the room: the one condition is that they cannot harm me. Or, to be more precise, they cannot leave visible marks on my body.

My body is a temple, the place they come to worship, repent, pray.

The wrist monitor informs me that working hours are over. I open the door and wander down the street, feeling the heat of all their gazes. They're like ant people looking up at a deity. They stare at me, every one of them, with a combination of sadness and joy, as though strug-gling to believe the image conjured by the light rays against their retinas—a flawless body, a body with hands, feet, and intact facial features. Eyes, ears, nose, mouth.

People able to remain in this city are almost all missing something. Arms, toes, ears. No one has done much research into why. Out on the street, everyone I encounter has something gone from their body, mostly legs and arms. I try to blend into the crowd and lopsided people sway around me, tilting forwards, tilting backwards, using one another for support. Bodies bump into bodies, shoulders rub against shoulders, like it's the most natural thing in the world. I keep my head down, speed up, move with the flow of the crowd, one step, another step, my limbs stiff. My stiffness is a weakness. When the other pedestrians detect my body among theirs, they move aside, clearing a path for me.

Their appearances don't hinder their daily lives too much. They go to work as normal, get off work as normal, go to eat in local diners, upload photos and videos to sharing platforms, make new friends online. Their mutilations are jigsaw puzzles: a cavity will always find a protuberance to fit it.

"A defect is an identifying feature. We upload the details to social media platforms and find others like us. If you haven't been on the app, maybe you don't know. I met a woman there who wouldn't even adopt a dog unless it had one eye, like she did. No other defect would do. Even a prosthetic eye was too much for her."

The shopkeeper chuckles to himself, his false eye observing me keenly, illustrating the city's hidden logic.

Once I met a man who, after he took off his shirt, suit trousers, and gloves, turned out to be mostly bone from the head down. Almost all his flesh was missing. He woke up one day to find he had somehow peeled it off in his sleep, although his backbone stayed strong enough to support his movements. While he slept, his sternum rose and fell protectively with his breath, the rhythm steady. His heart was big and powerful, sending blood to every far-flung corner of his body; I traced the lines of his arteries with my eyes, all those delicate streams of bright red blood. If you peeled the skin off a pig, the pig's heart would probably look much the same. I poked a finger behind this man's sternum and probed gently. What if one day, fast asleep, I inadvertently squeezed that lively little organ—would the man survive?

The wrist monitor strapped to his ulna said: Respiration rate average.

Over time, to be lacking something has become the defining feature of a person from this city. My intact body is increasingly conspicuous. My flawlessness has become my biggest flaw. I am obviously different, even if all people do is worship me for it.

They say I am grace.

"Impossible, just impossible."

The first time I met the shopkeeper, he was not yet a shopkeeper. Back then I called him Doctor.

I sat in his pristine white clinic, waiting. He was scrolling on his phone. His head remained lowered but his false eye rotated, scanning me, carrying out a series of checks. The computer was connected to my wrist monitor, scouring its stored data for signs of hidden illness. The screen showed that my heart rate and respiration were normal.

"There must be some mistake."

The shopkeeper (who was at that time the Doctor) ran the test again, his false eye spinning rapidly in its socket. Later, once I got to know him, I understood his spinning eye was like the wagging tail of a dog, speeding up when he got excited.

He reexamined my data several times. Then he asked me to lie down on his couch.

"It's simply miraculous. We're all losing things, and yet here you are, your body completely whole. Not a single mutilation! But you must know that people without defects cannot remain in the city."

He declared every single part of my body a miracle, worthy of a place in the record books. He asked me to leave, saying there was nothing he could do to help—not unless I myself knew of any hitherto unnoticed defect.

His right eye twinkled encouragingly. His left eye was unnaturally wide. When I replied to him, I focused only on the right one, on the eye I assumed he was born with, completely avoiding the left side of his face.

His eyes revolved towards his nose, as though following an invisible orbit. He reached a meaty hand to his right eye, his thumb and forefinger curled into a C, and then, without saying a word, as if all he were doing was taking off a pair of glasses, he plucked out the entire eyeball and dropped it into a glass of water.

I almost screamed. Not because his action pained me, but because it aroused in me an instant, thrilling sense of satisfaction, the opposite of fear.

"My vision was getting blurry."

The shopkeeper finally noticed my reaction. He glanced at my wrist monitor, looking a little apologetic.

Technology is too advanced, I thought. A false eye looks more natural than a natural one.

"You might not know this, but most people here refuse to wear prosthetics. They would rather preserve their damaged parts. Sometimes they even get satisfaction from them. They're not afraid of their defects; they're afraid of losing the desire to seek out what they have lost. To wear a false limb is to accept reality, to acknowledge the lack. Most people in this city still have so much hope. They're looking for you. You're their hope. They have hope that a body like yours still exists."

The shopkeeper's false eye blinked twice in the water, then revolved one hundred and eighty degrees, twinkling even more than it had earlier. I suddenly felt exhausted, but my watch wasn't telling me to sleep.

It had no instructions for me at all.

I said: "I'm lacking a job."

He gave me a room that was all bed, suitable for working, eating, sleeping. When the door was closed, the light was white and clear, penetrating every corner. The filth and the sordidness had nowhere to hide. I pressed my ear to the wall, hoping to hear giggles from next door, or even just rustling, but after fifteen minutes, I hadn't heard a single sound.

"Is the person next door someone like me?" I asked the shop-keeper, a little embarrassed. "I mean, is their body like mine?"

"No," he replied. "You're the only one like you. One day you'll get the chance to go next door."

I imagine I'm a doll. A doll for one hundred twenty minutes.

The man with the long face turns me over, then takes out a ruler. He's not here in pursuit of pleasure; he's here to experiment. In accordance with his advance requests, I lie on the bed without moving. Back to the ceiling, face to the floor. My vision thus restricted, I have to rely on the sensations when he touches me and the flickering of the light to guess what he's doing.

The pain is like sandpaper over my smooth arms. From the wet-ness I can tell it's a tongue.

His touch is like a cat's tongue. The man is crouched beside me with his tongue extended halfway. He's a cunning reptile, getting ready to swallow me whole. The faint stink of a stranger's saliva creeps over my body like an invisible snake. My back feels drenched. In accordance with the man's advance requests, I lie on the bed without mov-ing. His tongue inspects the peaks and valleys of my ear, then slides inside it, glacier sleek. His tongue reaches my pelvis and softens, dabs at my hipbones, slips lower. Then his tongue stops. He retracts it into his mouth. He stands up and takes a sip of water.

The shopkeeper calls this halftime, a malicious grin twitching at the corners of his mouth. In the second half, the man will get straight down to business.

The man does not expect resistance. I repress the urge to do the unexpected, waiting. His tongue grows more familiar with my body, sliding over me again and again, like an autopsy knife over a corpse. Before finishing, this stranger's tongue returns to my ear and swirls, one loop, another loop. The long-faced man's body heat steams up the room, and his moan of satisfaction echoes in my ear canal. I'm still lying face down on the bed, but I know he's made it, sunken now into murky white fantasy.

One time, the long-faced man doesn't leave when he should. I sit up. My neck cracks as I turn to face him and he instantly retreats, pressing himself into the wall joint like a lizard, turning away, refusing to look at me straight on.

As I put on my clothes, I see him in my peripheral vision, hunched over, hugging his knees as if trying to fold himself up.

When I go to open the door, I realize he doesn't want me to see his face. Both sides of his head are smooth as back muscles. The long-faced man has no ears.

People who have lost things always imagine that my body has something for them. That they'll find something here. A temporary prize.

The man with the long face never comes back, but the cat-tongue sensation remains stored in the memory of my wrist monitor. My skin still feels moist. Every now and then I open the saved information, to relive the experience.

I don't get the chance often, because here the days are long and the nights are short. Whenever I step outside on a break, the room next door is locked.

•

More people come here seeking help than go to doctors. They come to see me and project their hopes onto my body, lodge their hopes inside me, and then they wait eagerly for grace to be bestowed upon them.

After the black blindfold comes off, there's fluorescent white light. In it, I follow the instructions on my wrist monitor. I receive all manner of guests, and I satisfy all kinds of demands.

I lie on my back with my arms and legs in the air, pretending to be a dog in need of a belly scratch. I hold a middle-aged woman to my chest, allowing her to scrunch up her mouth like a baby and seek out my breast, nuzzling my areola. Over the course of sixty minutes, I promise her sixty times that I will never leave, that everything is good and whole. And with each reassurance, the first as much as the sixtieth, she lets out a mewl of satisfaction. I maintain the same intensity and posture throughout, re-creating precisely the same stroke sixty times over. My wrist monitor shows a satisfaction rating of 100 percent.

"What about afterward, do you ever think about them?"

I'm on a break, and the shopkeeper is asking me questions.

"For example, do you ever wonder why an old lady would want to bury her face in your breasts?"

I say that I don't.

"What about a grown man scratching your belly? Don't you think about that? You never want to ask why?"

I shake my head. Not only have I never thought to ask, I've never even thought about it in the first place. Until all these questions, I've never thought about much beyond the screen of my wrist monitor.

The shopkeeper isn't usually so chatty.

"Don't you think they're strange?" he continues. "They could do something about their defects, but they choose not to."

He's serious now. His eye socket is dark.

He follows me across the room. Closes the door. I adjust my monitor. The screen enters flight mode; this data is going unsaved.

I know what the shopkeeper wants. I'm not afraid he will hurt me. The mutilated dark hole on his face gives away his desires. The cavity is an endless gaze, concealing infinite yearning.

Inside the room, I believe I can do it. I can give him everything.

I hold my breath and open my eyes wide. With every touch—of his hands, of his tongue—my eyelids grow heavier, to the point that his satisfaction seems to decrease, even though he's smiling from ear to ear.

"You could try using your hair. The strands are so fine and your response reception area would be very large."

He stares off into space for a moment, then continues: "Your eyeballs would hurt, but with your hair you won't feel anything. Hair grows from follicles inside the skin; we have hundreds of thousands of strands of it, and inside each strand is a hair bulb which connects to our nerves and blood vessels. That's where hair comes from, and the hair bulb never stops growing, never stops producing new cells, never stops squeezing old cells out through the follicle."

I don't understand a word of what he's saying.

"Shall we keep going?"

He shakes his head.

"Your eyes are red, all full of veins. There are pluses and minuses to mutilation, you know. It makes certain things easier to handle."

He gets up to leave. He only has one remaining eye but, in it, his grief is plain to see. He's rushing now.

"Sometimes," he says, "I want to be like them and try to find pleasure in the absence. Maybe you'll start to feel this way too. You won't want to be left out anymore."

The door closes, and I'm alone in the room. My torn-off wrist monitor is silent. I lie blankly on the bed, staring at the ceiling, the shopkeeper's voice in my ears.

"Maybe you'll start to feel this way too. You won't want to be left out anymore."

People come and go, and the wrist monitor listens. It records their prayers. They squat beside the bed, they kneel at my feet. It isn't me they're seeing, even if their eyes are focused on me, gazing earnestly into my pupils, filling my eye sockets with all their hopes and emotions. In my body, they glimpse the possibility of wholeness, of no longer lacking anything.

The thought comes to me that, maybe, I want to feel something of the same consolation they derive from my body. That would be something real. Miraculous. That would be grace.

Next thing I know I'm standing outside the room next door. As I hesitate over whether or not to try the handle, I notice the door is ajar. A gentle nudge, and the room is revealed before me.

The same four walls. A floor plan exactly the same as mine, a mirror image. The same bright light. But there's nobody here, nobody at all.

On the bed there's a knife. Exactly the kind of sharp implement that would never appear on my side of the wall.

I pick up the knife. I pinch my eyelid in my left hand, pull the lid up, bring the knife in close to my eye. I hold my breath, stretch the lid out with my left hand, attack with my right hand, pierce, pull. My vision blurs, and the eyeball I have unmoored from my body bounces into the corner of the room.

I'm weaker now, but I keep going, keep cutting from my body—a little bit here, a little bit there, until the knife falls by itself from my hands.

I don't know how long I sleep.

A familiar voice pulls me from the darkness. The shopkeeper isn't talking to me; he's in the room collecting my hacked-off flesh, discarded arms, the soles of my feet. He's clutching all four of my limbs, muttering to himself.

"How careless! The empathy setting was too high, it tipped into self-mutilation mode, a desire for approval . . . now, where did that eyeball get to?"

I want to give him one last clue. To tell him that the liquid seeping from that eyeball in the corner is tears.

Translator's Note

Samwai and I were matchmade for this piece by the Hong Kong poet Nicholas Wong. All he told me beforehand was that the story had come out of a writing workshop based on "body movements," and that he thought we might find common ground in queerness. I think this is all a reader needs to know going in, perhaps along with a reminder to consider how Hong Kong has a body, too.

[I have a collection of powerful objects]

Jesús Amalio Lugo
translated from the Spanish by David M. Brunson
Copper Nickel

I have a collection of powerful objects
from different celestial sources
a rosary of fluorescent plastic
a letter from my dead father
various birthday cards
a pearl that is the moon—only my friends and I know—
a paraplegic turtle named Vértigo who sleeps beside my cousin
a compass that, in spite of magnetism, points south
and a notebook where I try—truthfully—to write without liter-
    ary intentions
All of my objects are legacies of God
What is God?
I get a bit tangled up when explaining my faith
What if I'm an atheist? I don't believe, because I believe
My beliefs are so many that I might have messianic tendencies
I believe:
I believe in the effectiveness of my sister Miriam praying the
    rosary in the middle of three P.M. traffic
I believe in the certainty of my other sister—Milagro—who
    believes she speaks with God
when she closes her eyes
I believe in my mother taming enemies with her holy card of the
    Lion Saint

I believe in Nadia's Buddhism
God works better if we breathe from the belly
I believe in Bach's flowers
calluna vulgaris and mimulus guttatus
in more chocolate, four times a day, before sleep
I believe in the aging women who dance like teenagers every
    Thursday at seven
I believe in Mrs. Aida and her Sunday prayers in Maravén
I believe in the tasks that my father entrusts me when I dream
I believe that, when I was eleven, I saw a fairy trapped in the
    power lines in front of my house
And yes, I confess before you brothers of science and power
that I believe in a pair of Bible verses
and two or three poetry collections
No, I am not religious
but when they sing my country's anthem, it's like prayer
When I speak of my people, and their Marquezian situations
I preach
When I speak of my friends and family
—with their divine eccentricities—
I am not an immigrant, I am a missionary
Because God is all of the people that love me
God is all of those I love
And if my name is Jesús, it's because my father is God
as are my mother and my sisters
Jehová, Yavé, Patricia, Mariana
Angélica, Aneidis, and Ana
So numerous are their names
Uncountable their miracles
No, I am not religious, but each of their words is a new verse in
    my testament

A moment with them: another aggregate to my sacred memory
That's why I ask you lord
that if, for having a sinful and reckless mind,
I fall back into hell
protect the many hands that would burn
to lift me out

Translator's Note

Owing to an ongoing human rights crisis driven by the country's authoritarian government, corruption, violent crime, and food shortages, over seven million people have fled Venezuela. Of these people, five million have remained in the Americas. Though this is the world's second-largest refugee crisis (trailing just behind Russia's invasion of Ukraine), there has been a remarkable lack of institutional response, with governments instead choosing to create insurmountable bureaucratic obstacles for displaced Venezuelans, effectively locking them out of the system and restricting access to residency, regular work, housing, healthcare, and other basic human rights, all contrary to UN member nations' obligations under the 1951 "Convention Relating to the Status of Refugees."

Lamentably, this is also true in Chile, where at least 440,000 (and probably many more undocumented) Venezuelans have started new lives, despite many of these bureaucratic obstacles. Jesús Amalio Lugo is among them. His poem "[I have a collection of powerful objects]" is born of the tragedy of contemporary Venezuela. These are objects connected to the speaker's homeland. All carry with them the weight of loss—of family, of place, of direction. Though the poem recognizes the brutality of Venezuela ("If . . . I fall back into hell"), rather than remain in this space, the speaker instead chooses to celebrate Venezuelan identity in the face of this adversity. Through the unshakable ties of family, memory, and culture, the poem elevates the experience of immigration into the realm of the holy: "I am not an immigrant, I am a missionary." Reading and translating this poem, I, for one, am proselytized.

Death, Peppermint Flavored

Ashur Etwebi
translated from the Arabic by James Byrne and Ashur Etwebi
Michigan Quarterly Review

Sleep is the stem of a peppermint.
It can only be seen horizontally.

Sleep is the roundness of the universe. Sleep is a stretched
    courtyard.
Sleep, the jar of language. Sleep, a box of photographs.
Sleep, the crown seal.

Sometimes, facing the sun,
the hands of sleep became a sofa where every creature sat.

It's difficult to choose between a bird and a bull.
The bird spreads its wings in a vast sky,
and the bull carries the sun tirelessly.

Difficult to choose between wearing my clothes or wearing
    nakedness.
A door is cleverer than me, it has two hearts.

Often, I feel my sleep is like rain,
and my desire is song tangled in the beaks of birds.
I am like a robe hanging from a crack in the sky.

On the wall of night, I lay down my blues.

To ascend or descend. Choices I neither take, nor leave behind.

Translators' Note

Ashur Etwebi and James Byrne first met in 2009 and subsequently translated much of *Five Scenes from a Failed Revolution* (Arc, 2022) in Svalbard, the nearest inhabited archipelago to the North Pole. At the time, Etwebi was forced to find political asylum in Norway after he was attacked and his house was burned down by a militia in Libya. Byrne writes: "Ashur and I first met at a poetry festival in Syria and became quick friends. We met again a couple of years after this when both he and Khaled Mattawa—the most notable Libyan poets alive today—invited me to participate in Tripoli's first international literary festival post-Gaddafi. In Libya, Ashur became a target for those who feel internationalism represents a collusion with the West. At the time I met him in Syria, I hadn't realized what a major literary figure Etwebi is. Given his prolific output and his range as a writer, it would be reductive to label him a 'political poet'. He is the survivor of a traumatic experience echoing on and sometimes these echoes reverberate through the poems. Quite often the effect of this is subtle (poetry is 'bubbles floating from the fins of a fish'); other times it is more direct (the blue morning carries 'bullets of ignorant militias'). Ashur's is an open and enquiring poetics; meditative, lush with metaphor and imagery."

Our Village

Tesfamariam Woldamarian
translated from the Tigrinya by Charles Cantalupo
   and Menghis Samuel
Guernica

You say, our village.
Do you mean our exact village,
The one we saw at dawn,
Where we watched the sunrise
And spent the morning,
The afternoon,
And the evening,
And where we stayed?

If you really mean
This village,
It has a village underneath,
And a village under that

Before the modern one you see:
A village before Islam;
Another village before Christianity;
Yet another before the kingdom
Of the Jews;
And one before the worship of the sun;
Yet another
Before the deities of anyone.

You say, our village.
Exactly which one out of these?
Our village is a veteran of
So many histories
That if you want to know
About the one below
Or about the one above
You have to say the number
Counting up or down.

You say, our village,
But is it at night,
Twilight, midnight?
The village where we sleep,
The village where we wake
At sunrise,
Or at the dawn of history?
All at once they make

One massive ladder
With endless rungs
Through vast and countless
Levels upon levels
Outspreading up and down,
Set deeply in eternity
To rise
Beyond the skies.

You say, our village, but
In relation to what?
The village has a village

Behind it and before;
To the right, in the middle,
On the left, and more
Villages beyond.
Our village runs the range:
From traditional, to hidebound,
To life in balance, and to change.

You say, our village, but
Merely numbering the districts
In the province looks
Like counting pages in a book
That should be read instead.
Step by step and inch by inch
Our village and our home
Is like our nation—
Exceeding any sum of its parts.

So, you say, our village.
Exactly which one?
Our village of the past,
Our village here, today,
The modern wannabe,
Or the village you can't see,
And the village that will really be
Modern, even postmodern?

Translators' Note

Tesfamariam Woldemariam's 2014 book, ህያው ደብሪ (*Hiyaw Debri* or "The Living Monastery"), confirmed him as Eritrea's greatest modern poet. Brought out by Hdri Publishers, this critically annotated collection spanned three hundred pages. Like Beyene Haile, Eritrea's greatest modern novelist, with whom Tesfamariam was often compared, his work offered an unprecedented blend of personal and political passion, fresh and original language, dazzling poetic form, intriguing difficulty, and disarming simplicity to express the essence of Eritrea to its people and the world.

In Asmara in 2017, Charles Cantalupo first heard about Tesfamariam from an Eritrean colleague, the leading intellectual and historian Zemhret Yohannes, who directed Hdri Publishers and the country's national archives. At the same time, another longtime colleague there, Menghis Samuel, who was also Tesfamariam's friend and one of his most devoted readers, told Charles about his poetry. They decided to try to translate it. Translating Eritrean poets for twenty years, Charles felt like it took that long to be trusted with such a national treasure. It took Menghis and him four years to produce *The Living Monastery* of their own: an abridged, bilingual edition of the original. Yet the challenge of Tesfamariam required them to work so closely, continuously, and intensely—Menghis in Asmara and Charles in Bethlehem, Pennsylvania—that their back-and-forth process amounted to a book length dialogue, not only on relating to Tesfamariam's unique poetic achievement but also on the nature of translation and poetry, which they will also publish.

The Sea Krait

Enrique Villasis
translated from the Filipino by Bernard Capinpin
Washington Square Review

1.

Newly molted, it descended to the waters. In its new life, it established itself in the sea. It left its apprehensions by the shore with its old skin. It had no view in the deep aside from the slumbering darkness: stones and dead coral were skulls of an unfathomable beast which later heaved and yawned as the undertow swept. It hoped that an eel might dart out from the crevices. What else was venom for? Solitude was far more fatal.

2.

All it wanted most was to find companionship. Here was a pile of old skin, a recognizable repugnance. The gash it got by slipping on an old rock didn't even heal. As before, it started again to believe in uncertainty.

3.

The humid sea was blooming on his skin, here, at the surface of a wide stone, at the mouth of a cave. It chose to stay. Not far off, the sound of the chord and the eastern wind flocking. A hat flapping, there was a chill in the wind when it flew, and among the waves, it will be one with its own reflection. It's easy to say that each gust was proof to the existence of spite, that there were angels that crossed the mind, picking up unfulfilled wishes, collecting and releasing them as whirlwinds or typhoons. Meanwhile, the sea krait will endure the overgrowth of hisses: a cry like in a duet. Only then could it feel its own breath again.

4.

An old legend: a sage was caged and hung on the oldest mangrove tree from a distant island. His crime was that he taught the old prayers to the parrots. It was there he learned that one could write on a living krait's skin. Every night after writing, he was afflicted by a fever: a part of his soul was inscribed in the very letters scraped and peeled from the sea snake's scales, and he would watch it swim farther away. At the center of his eye, the words glistened in the heat and brine. This was the only way he knew how to quench a desire shawled by sorrow.

He charted the map underneath his prison, and like a cartographer, he plotted the landmarks according to their own purpose and history, and every so often, he determined it by the movement of his shadow and reflection. So his city below a mirror took no permanent order. In truth, his revulsion erased its origin, loneliness flowed beneath the bones. One time, he jotted down the first unanswered riddle: blind when caught, sees when held.

Fate, how simple it's supposed to be.

5.

After a few months, a reply came, which like him was written on the sea krait's skin: Like the venom from first discovering fire, I was left unable to breathe. I hate you because I couldn't speak.

6.

The sage's townsfolk came back to him. After the storm, the parrots he taught returned, and spoke in the tone of their god, in accursed screeches. Some grew blisters on their index fingers. Some torn open by the frequency of their pitch. There was one who heard nothing in his mind except the repetitive sound of stone splashing on water. In the end, they accepted their mistake. But the sage was not there. Only an abandoned cage reeking of molted hide. It stuck to the air. Who else could they beg for forgiveness? Who could they ask for wisdom?

A time came when two sea kraits were found caught in a fishing net. One entwined in another. On their skins, a message was etched:

You were like a country that had abandoned me—with nothing prepared for me except silence. In my travels, I found myself asking: in the end, which baggage will become part of myself? I've discarded everything since, and when I turned around, I found a wandering owl which, like me, kept questioning.

And even with such few words, the second message seemed to hold an answer.

Each one of us carries a burden. Amidst a thousand bubbles, you will find yourself: immaculate and bare.

Translator's Note

This poem is part of the author's first book of poems, *Agua*, which he describes as a sort of bestiary of sea creatures in the Philippines. For this piece, I want to capture the palpability of the images, some borrowed from Milorad Pavić's novel *Dictionary of the Khazars*, and to transpose into English the undulating rhythms of the original.

A Red Blight

Juan Cárdenas
translated from the Spanish by Lizzie Davis
Los Angeles Review of Books

Now I'd like to touch briefly on the surreal apparition of a bridge. It must have been '95, the start of the summer after we finished high school. My friend Chino and I were headed down a yellow dirt road, and who was that coming up behind us? Milena and her friends, of course—their names, I don't remember. We were on our way back from the campesino co-op, we'd gone for cans of tuna, some eggs, a crate of Póker beer. Chino and I were doing our best to carry it all. We had to stop now and then, because we were skinny, the both of us, and not very tall; we'd set the crate on the ground and mop off our sweat with our dusty forearms. This sun isn't fucking around, Chino said, and the girls, I can see it now, they climbed up a tree, the guamas were ripe, and we acted like we couldn't see their legs. Come on! Chino yelled, but they ignored him, kept eating the cottony skin of the fruit, throwing black seeds at us, laughing, ridiculous. YOU COME ON, YOU PUSSIES! yelled Milena, who was like that, precocious, and always got carried away. We ignored her too. We just waited for them to finish doing their thing up in the guama branches, and let the wind circle us, pulling along their laughter and the shouts of some campesinos who played soccer there that time of day, up on the field in front of the co-op. Chino observed that the river was very low. Summer's giving its all, he said, but we can still swim at Monte Agraz, no problem, and even jump off the cliffs, you'll see. Monte Agraz was the land Chino's family owned. That's where we were, our minds elsewhere, when we heard a motorbike coming along.

It was Pipo on his Yamaha 175. On the back was a guy we called Bofe who never cracked a smile. He only laughed on the inside, like he was swallowing up his laughter, and no one knew a thing about him or his life except for Pipo, who went all over the place with Bofe and would have fought anyone for him. Pipo stopped at the foot of the guama and, motor still on, he started to chat up the girls. Eventually, he offered to take one, whoever wanted to go, to Monte Agraz. Get off, Bofe, he said. And Bofe obeyed so that, obviously, Milena could get on, and the other two even hid any hint that they wished they were in her place. Pipo and Milena blazed by, and two seconds later they vanished behind the first curve in the road. The other two shuffled over, as if whipped by Milena's display of power. Chino had gone over to the riverbank to look for a piece of bamboo we could slide through the crate handles, so we could carry the beer on our shoulders. The girls couldn't make up their minds: first we were two costaleros carrying floats for Semana Santa, then two servants carrying white people's luggage in *Tarzan*. It was easier to carry like that, but we still had to stop and rest sometimes. Bofe followed behind, not a word came out of him, mug fixed right on the ground. His presence was so subtle the girls hardly noticed him.

An hour later, we got to the entrance to Monte Agraz, shirts soaked with sweat. Pipo, Milena, and four other nobodies, who'd snuck their way in who knows how, were half naked already, laying out poolside, music cranked all the way up. Vallenatos, which is what people listened to then. The start of an era, you could say, the era of teenagers with pool water up to their waists, the bottle of guaro held high, those ragged vocals, too sentimental, love as a barricade hiding . . . I don't know what, hiding something. Now we know the notes of the vallenato are written in barbed wire around land irrigated with blood, but back then they still seemed like an innocent demonstration of lightness. Pure show. Didn't the Pythagoreans say we should fear a change in music taste more than a change in administration? Well, that's what it was, what they were, those kids, those vallenateros— they knew all the lyrics by heart, and they sang them, almost scream- ing, and drank guaro from small plastic cups. A musical change of regime.

The only ones not singing, or half singing just for sociability's sake, were Chino and me. And Bofe, because back then, we still didn't know what music he liked, or if he liked music at all. In the span of a couple years, Chino and I had gone from techno and house to punk, but since we were too provincial and proud to admit that we still liked electronic music and dance music, we publicly declared ourselves rabid enemies of anything with synths. And, against all odds, there we were, standing out but sitting on the edge, legs stuck in icy water. It was that or what Bofe was doing: playing loner beneath a plantain tree. Chino and I were holding out hope that one of those girls would look at us the way they'd been looking at Pipo, and another one of the heartthrobs, a tall blond kid who always dressed well, even there, in the middle of nowhere: shorts and sandals, yeah, but a nice floral shirt up top, and he slid down his sunglasses over and over, just to show off his blue eyes. Neither Chino nor I had mastered that kind of flirtation. To tell you the truth, we'd mastered no flirtation at all. We had no idea how to catch anyone's eye, but it's true there was something classy in that: we were patient, and we assumed that no one would touch us, not with a ten-foot pole.

That afternoon, I made a big pot of tuna pasta for everyone, and when it got a little later, because the sun was still beating down on us, and because Chino insisted, we decided to go off in search of the famous swimming holes. We walked a long time, crossed cof- fee fields and pastures, and then we came to the tracks of a train that hadn't been through in forty years at least. There was a nobleness to those ruins, the old wooden cross ties, the stretches of rail that

hadn't been carried off yet, to sell as scrap. There was a tract of at
least two kilometers where Chino's parents were running a brujita
—a little witch, that's what they call handcars over there. We piled
onto the wooden platform, and Pipo and Bofe grabbed either end of
the lever and set the brujita in motion. We weren't moving very fast,
but it was nice going down the tracks on an improvised flying carpet.
One of Milena's friends had been glued to her wannabe boyfriend
the whole time. They'd been talking soft to each other. I listened in
and was surprised to hear them going on about biology—birds, to
be precise, a topic I also found interesting. The girl abruptly changed
the subject, murmured something about starting college: she was
finding it hard to get her dad on board with the major, he of course
had hoped she'd pick something useful, with better prospects. The
kid let out a sharp laugh and said maybe he was better off fatherless.
The girl gave him a tight smile, she didn't know what to say, so the
wannabe had to explain himself: my mom raised my brother and me
on her own, we have no idea who our dad is, but it's no difference.
Plus, he said, we're not highschoolers anymore. Everything's going
to change when we get to college and stop being a bunch of brats.
That, everyone on the brujita could hear. Minutes passed, and no
one said a thing. Then Pipo tried to talk us into another vallenato,
but no one jumped in to humor his wounded-male howling. Real
pals you are, he said, and there was nothing for him to do but keep
pushing the lever in silence, till we got to the end of the track. From
there on out, there were no rails, not even sleepers, and the yellow
path looked like a toothless gum.

We kept on that defanged path for a while, sometimes pushing
through mountains of brush that sprung up in ditches left by the rails,
and it was then that I realized I was surrounded by little impromptu
pairs. The two who'd been talking about birds, of course; but also
Chino and Blue Eyes; Pipo and his faithful Bofe; Milena and the other
guy. At the end of the line, stragglers, maybe up to something, still

laughing nonstop, the two girls who'd lobbed guama seeds at us that morning. I didn't have a match. Suddenly, I was alone. I hurried to latch onto Chino, who'd already started to sermonize to the other guy about Argentinian rock, its obvious superiority. Come on, don't think twice about it, he said. Mexico, Spain, Brazil, that's not rock. It might be good music, but it's not *rock*. The stud in the floral shirt, who'd already used up the technique of peeling off his sunglasses to reveal the blue mirage, tried to convince him otherwise. But Chino was walking all over him. It was obvious the stud knew nothing of rock, much less Argentinian rock, and he barely managed to throw out some overworked names. At one point, I wanted to jump in, show them that I knew my way around, but, I don't know why, I couldn't open my mouth, and after that, I felt a little weird. Then I tried to attach myself to the girls at the tail end of us, but no way there, either. I was alone, without a pair, for almost the rest of the day. And when we finally got to that swimming hole, I made up my mind to dive off the top of a cliff where Chino's parents had a plank halfway suspended in the void: a makeshift trampoline. Later I swam to the opposite shore of the river to lie on a rock. I was basically throwing a tantrum to get anyone's attention, but still no one noticed.

The pairs were having fun and I, resigned to solitude, tanned my puny body; as Milena had said, *you're a pussy.* For two years I'd been trying to build muscle, exercising, eating tons of protein, but all of that just gave me acne and depression and more acne. A strange acne, coming and going, not the typical rash, the huge pores, but gigantic balls of blocked oil that sometimes covered my nose or my forehead, impervious to all creams. I just had to wait, sometimes months, and grow out my hair so it covered my face. No, not thin. Scrawny. Spotted. But at least you have interesting hair. That's what I said to myself while the sun stuck my bones to the bank. I had a rockero's hair. It could have been worse. And the permanent depression gave me an interesting aura. That's how I attempted to cheer myself up back then, in that sad period when I tried everything, even Mom's makeup, to cover my blemishes. There were days when I showed up to school caked in foundation, like Edward Scissorhands, and at first they all made cruel jokes, but eventually they accepted it, the way you come to respect somebody's illness. That hurt a lot more than the jokes. Once, lining up at the store on our break, I heard one classmate say to another, So you really think he likes guys? And when they saw it was me behind them, they froze, and they had to make a huge effort to even half cover it up.

I pretended like nothing had happened and made it all the way through the line to buy the greasy food that would supposedly toughen me up.

At the end of break, shut up in one of the bathroom stalls, I came to a few conclusions: they thought I liked guys because of the makeup, but they also thought that was too bad, because I had a nice face. I tried not to take it too hard, but that afternoon I couldn't get out of bed. Not the next day, either, or the next . . . I spent two full months half-asleep, lying in my bedroom, headphones blasting music. And that's how I felt now, sun beating down on me, imagining my cartilage was liquefying already, to fuse with the rock. I'm skinnier than a mosquito, I was thinking. Luckily, on those summer days, my acne almost disappeared. Maybe I was becoming an adult, like the aspiring biologist said. Maybe something was finally changing for the better in my body.

On the way back, I forced myself out of my mental hideout and toward the conversation Milena was having. She'd changed pairs and was now discussing real estate with Pipo. Milena was bragging that her family didn't have land. My dad is a businessman, what we have is houses. One here and another in Cali. But land, no, she said, what for. My dad says that's just a money pit, 'cause farming has no future in this country. And especially not around here, where the campesinos live off the backs of everyone else and just want the land to sit around on it, scratching their balls. I mean, that's what my dad says. I think he's probably right. Pipo nodded, a little confused, because he agreed with part of that, and part, he disagreed with, and his family, a family of surnames and bloodlines, owned a huge swath of land, they'd been accumulating land, it was said, since the eighteenth century. In fact, to some people, the name "Pipo" was synonymous with enslavement, gold mines on the Pacific coast, notorious haciendas, though there was only a shadow of all that left: some properties as sprawling as they were useless, take the cattle away, and there's nothing. For all those reasons, he had no response for Milena, so he hurried to take shelter in a less threatening conversation.

When we were alone, Milena asked if my family had land, and I said no, that my family had been very poor until my parents made some money and we became middle, maybe upper-middle, class. My grandma only finished third grade, to give you an idea, I said. And Chino? she asked. How come he has land? Is Chino Chinese? I was quick to explain that Chino wasn't Chinese, his mother was Japanese. The land had belonged to his grandfather on his dad's side, a military guy in Santander de Quilichao or something like that. Her interest in the subject of property faded fast, and we started jumping from one thing to another. Milena was obsessed with motorcycles. I knew nothing about motorcycles, but I paid attention while she rattled off cylinder capacities, makes, motocross racers she'd dated or partied with in Cali on the weekends. For her, there was nothing sweeter in life than a motocross race featuring, you guessed it, Camilo Reina, which rolled off her tongue like one word, "camilorreina." Then she confessed she'd done coke for the first time with camilorreina the year before, and all those motocross guys did their races high out of their minds, coked up, assholes and all, because they jumped higher that way, it made them more aggressive. I didn't know much about drugs, either—Chino and I had smoked weed a few times, that was it—so I asked her what it was like. Milena answered without hesitation that she had a bag right there, and if I wanted, I could try some. I was so excited, and also scared, that I started to shake, but I didn't want to come off like a prude, so I said, Let's do it, how?

First, we let all those narks get ahead, she said, showing the whites of her eyes as if we were plotting a murder, and I knew that it wasn't her gesture, that it was copied from somebody else. Surely that's how she'd been offered it her first time, like being invited into a kind of satanic ritual. When they get back on the brujita, we'll tell them we're coming behind, she said, that we're going to walk, and we'll cut through the field. And that's what we did. All the others got on the brujita, operated again by the group's two strongmen, and Milena and I cut through an empty pasture where the grass had shot up. This finca is, like, abandoned, she said. She was nervous about snakes.

I told her that Chino's family's business had been way down for years, actually, ever since Chino's mom died, because she was the one who managed their money and kept it all in order. Chino's dad is pretty much useless. He's thrown all their money down the drain, I think, bad investments or something. There's no one to manage the farm anymore, or to cook or clean the house, they can't pay anybody. We had to clean the pool ourselves yesterday. You wouldn't believe it, it was all full of spiderwebs and feathers, a bat had drowned in there too. Nasty! Milena said, hopping around like she was dodging creepy-crawlies.

She was happy we were nearing the end of the pasture. Then we entered a coffee field I'd never seen, the entirety of the old crop eaten away by fungi, the ground covered in rotten produce, forest already taking back some terrain. We even saw little squirrels hopping between the branches of guayacans. It's already getting overgrown, said Milena. We're lucky we haven't seen any mutts, or worse.

Almost involuntarily, we were drawn by the sound of the river, which, there, was very rocky, the current strong. We walked along on the bank, and she looked for the perfect place. This is good, she said finally, pointing at a rock that looked more like a king-sized bed, under the shade of two guaduas. With some ceremony, we settled on the smooth surface, finding lotus pose like two Tibetan monks about to jump into the bardo, and started doing bumps off the tip of a key. I was filled with false joy, grating euphoria, pain muffled like an LP spinning in the neighbor's apartment. But combined, all those discomforts were enjoyable, in the long run, pleasant. She asked how I was feeling, and I tried to sum it up: bad and good and bad and then good again. But good. From Milena's mouth escaped a slippery laugh that jumped from stone to stone, and it was in that moment, trying to follow its skipping downriver, because it really was like her laugh had described the space we were sitting in, the tunnel of vegetation growing between shallow cliffs, it was then that, I kid you not, we both saw the bridge, its legs spread, at the back of the landscape. It seems like a total lie, I know, like something out of never-never land. But in the light that came through the wavering foliage, the bridge shone, the way they say certain animals shine on the hunt. The golden prey that offers itself to the noble and somewhat distracted hunter. What the fuck is that? Milena said. And I didn't know what to say back.

The whole situation was too much for me, it seemed measureless. We sat there and took in the vision of that magical bridge for a while, I can't say how long, maybe half an hour, or maybe just five long minutes. We didn't even think about going over to get a better look. We both knew that if we moved around too much, the bridge would flee like a scared animal, so we focused on just admiring it: it was beautiful and strange, a suspension bridge made of vines that had grown almost on a whim to claim its bamboo frame and rungs of fine ruined wood. We thought we noticed that bag of bones breathing, exhaling a red blight over the living foliage. And for a second, I almost couldn't help but ask Milena: Do you love me? Are you in love with me? With me, in spite of everything? But I didn't say a word, of course not. I bit my lip and held on, mouth shut. No one with any tact would ruin a moment like that with such a stupid question. She was the one who grabbed my hand and spoke: It's OK, she said, her voice very sweet, childlike from the cocaine, it's OK. It'll pass really quickly, you'll see.

Translator's Note

For authors, I suspect that being translated sometimes feels like traveling back in time, to a previous version of themselves and their writing. There's often a lag between the publication of an original and its translation into English: translations comprise a notoriously small percentage of literary publications in the U.S., and presses can require abundant "evidence" of a book's worthiness before commissioning one—the kind of evidence (publicity, sales numbers, prizes) that can take years to accumulate. When I met Juan Cárdenas, he had published five books, none yet available in English. By the time my second Cárdenas translation appears on shelves, six years after its initial release, Juan will have published his eighth book in Spanish.

I share this because "A Red Blight" was my first opportunity to translate something almost simultaneously to Juan's writing it. I received it while working on a novel he had published in Spanish in 2017, and it accelerated me into his 2022 prose. "A Red Blight" at first seemed quite distinct from the Cárdenas novels I was familiar with: in contrast to their polyvocality, formal ambitiousness, and sometimes baroque prose style, it features a single narrator who seems to address the reader, a simpler structure, and conversational language. The experience of reading it was unusual, like seeing someone after a long absence and noticing all at once how they've changed. But one aspect of the text felt very familiar, and I used it to guide my approach: like Juan's earlier long-form fiction, "A Red Blight" is marked by a keen attention to sound and rhythm, which here he happens to channel in service of an off-the-cuff orality.

Translating it was a chance not only to jump forward and meet Juan in time, but also to deepen my engagement with one element of his writing that persists across its evolution.

Deterioration

Fatemeh Shams
translated from the Persian by Armen Davoudian
Poetry Northwest

On that day which is still today all your verbs changed to the past:
forty-one years living in each other's arms
until today, when one of us is here and yet is not
in this house, where imaginary interrogators invade memories of
    lovemaking
and this neck, which everyday trembles at the prospect of the noose
and these eyes, which almost black out scanning the corners of the
    room for cats

Forty-one years until today, when one of us is here but the other is
    not
in a house where heavenly angels of death toy with memories of
    childhood
and this locked mouth, no longer in search of an excuse to laugh or
    kiss

On that day which is still today you lost all sense of verb tense:
—*The guests are still here, they have not left*
—*The guests would like some tea*
—*The guests will take me with them*
—*The guests took me with them to be hanged . . . are taking . . . will take*

Every day:
pouring tea for your executioners
ordering kebab for your executioners
staring into the eyes of your executioners
writing a letter of confession for your executioners

Every day:
forgetting familiar names to make room for the names of your
        imaginary executioners
forgetting familiar bodies to flee from delirious shadows

Every day:
a day which is still today
a day when your present condition will be summed up
in the simple conjugation of a tenseless verb
in your dumb, timeless tongue.

Translator's Note

I was first drawn to Fatemeh Shams's poetry in part because of her unapologetic embrace of heterogeneous styles, from classical ghazals to politically charged free verse to surrealist prose poems. Her inclusive poetics, prodigal and exacting at once, lingers over questions of exile, sexual repression, and the intrusion of public into private life. In "Deterioration," a private illness becomes a powerful metaphor for the malaise of a whole nation. Herself in exile in the U.S., the poet imagines her childhood home in Mashhad, where her father suffers from Parkinson's disease. Gradually, as the poem goes on, it becomes difficult to tell the difference between the symptoms of Parkinson's and everyday life under an oppressive regime, where the threat of raids fosters an atmosphere of paranoia. These symptoms, while painfully literal, also come to resemble, strangely, the conditions of exile, as memories of life in the native country and one's mastery of the native tongue face the threat of gradual deterioration.

Bone

Behçet Necatigil
translated from the Turkish by Neil P. Doherty
The Antonym

And into the ceilings seeps a smell of tallow
From the candles so quietly quenched
And people looking right looking left
In haste bury something so nobody sees at all
And then down the long boulevard they run

And at night from the flocks a sheep goes missing
And people looking right looking left pass
In haste cross over one last time before they die
Then later in solitude they sit and lick
A very old bone they'd plucked from the walls

Translator's Note

In 2015 I was invited by Saliha Paker to take part in that year's Cunda International Workshop for Translators of Turkish Literature. Each year a certain poet was chosen and various translators were invited to work on translating their poetry. When I was told that we would be working on Behçet Necatigil I was thrilled, as he was one of the major Turkish poets I had shied away from translating up to that point. I had always been fascinated by his work but found it dense and mysterious. In the months before the workshop, I read as much of his poetry as I could and saw that when translating him I would need to develop a "Necatigil language" within English, one parallel to what he had done in Turkish. This meant condensing as much as possible and shuffling the word order around in order to recreate the startling effects of the original. This involved a process of translating and retranslating until the translation took on a certain Necatigil aura, one that managed to make English seem strange and yet somehow fresh again.

Rune Poems from Bergen, Norway, Thirteenth and Fourteenth Century

by an unknown author
translated from the runic alphabet by Eirill Alvilde Falck
Poetry

MONOSTICH IN RUNES, ETCHED ON WOOD

My love : kiss me

─────

DISTICH IN RUNES, ETCHED ON WOOD IN TWO PIECES

remember : me : I : remember : you
love : me : I : love : you

─────

DESIDERIUM IN RUNES, ETCHED ON WOOD

I love a wife not mine
I will leave her
when mountains walk
:
wisewoman, how we love
rends the Earth
:

I will leave her
when ravens pale
:
pale as the snow
on migrating mountains

Translator's Note

The first word I ever translated was my name. I painted it onto a piece of cloth during art class at my elementary school.ᛙᛁᚱᛁᚿ. I was fascinated with the sharp lines of the letters, with learning they appeared as they did because of the way they were produced—sharp tools cutting into unyielding surfaces.

In 1955, a fire destroyed large parts of the harbor district in Bergen, Norway. In its wake, archeological excavations uncovered hundreds of objects with runic inscriptions. The find revealed that runes were used for more than purely formal purposes. Many of the inscriptions were akin to text messages or graffiti, others to short poems. Some were romantic or erotic or both.

Runic inscriptions, however short or casual, never feel short or casual. There is always the knowledge of the way they came into being—slowly, with strain, with sharp objects. A complete poem: My love : kiss me.

The Funeral

Geet Chaturvedi
translated from the Hindi by Anita Gopalan
Two Lines

Stars shine in the eyes of old princesses, too, I thought, watching Rosa Aunty standing in a fresh, polka-dotted frock before the clinical, slabbed steps of the Asiatic Library. Head back, she was gazing intently at the library. Her frail, pallid coloring complemented that vast, milky whiteness gleaming, resplendent, in the clear nine o'clock sun. On a normal day, we could hardly find any space for our feet, but today, there were no feet apart from ours. The air was thick with the lethargic reticence of an unhurried Sunday.

Once we'd climbed out of the black-and-yellow Mumbai taxi, she'd handed me her bag, and the two of us stood this way for some time before she began mounting the library steps, very slowly, gripping me with her left hand, her cane with her right.

On the fifth step, she paused. "How many have we climbed?" she asked breathlessly.

"Five."

A moment later, she continued the ascent, her bony hand tightly wound over mine.

"Now?"

"This is the tenth step."

She turned and climbed down one step.

"Count again. This would be the ninth step, no?"

I launched into a performance of loudly counting each step and affirmed cheerfully, "Yeah, the ninth."

From up there, we looked down toward the street. Despite not being very high, we now had a panoramic view of the street below. Slowly, steadily, she sidled, cane clacking, all the way to the right edge of the steps, at which point she released my hand and motioned for me to sit. I carefully lowered her down before squatting beside her in the space to her right. Our bottoms were resting on the ninth step. Smoothing out her frock, she stretched her legs, her heels propped on the seventh step. Like a restless pigeon cocking its head, she scanned the odd banalities of our surroundings.

A vehicle or two whizzed past intermittently. Her eyes would chase them until they disappeared beyond view. She took her bag from me and fumbled with its contents before taking out a small lunch box.

"You don't look eighteen," she said, setting the bag aside. She was looking at me intently, her eyes kind.

"I'm fourteen," I said pleasantly.

"Oh! You're four years away." I detected a note of surprise beneath her words.

I smiled at her, more out of habit than anything else.

Then, as if startled into consternation, she said, "But—but why are you sitting on this side? You should be on this side," and, pointing to her other side, "C'mon, get up. Come over to my left."

I never tried to understand her oddities. So I rose obediently and took my place on her left. As if these were our natural places.

She slid sideways and leaned against the balustrade. I remained squatting in my assigned place. Looking at the distance between us, she said, "Come closer, not so far away." I moved closer. "Places have great importance in life," she said. "The world we see depends on where we are perched." I smiled at this succinct, philosophical sort of statement, as she opened her lunch box. In it were two sandwiches, with a spangle of red cherry on top. She wrapped one in tissue paper and handed it to me. "Eat."

I opened my mouth wide and, voracious, bit off a huge chunk. "Eat slowly," she warned, though not unkindly.

Embarrassed, I suddenly became self-conscious. Bowing my head, I tried to control the speed at which I gorged myself. When I finished, she said, "If you're still hungry, you can eat my sandwich as well."

"No, I'm done," I said, wiping my lips with the tissue paper, to which she responded with a vague, faraway smile. For a while after, her lunch box lingered open. Perhaps she was waiting for me to snatch her share. We didn't have any further conversation. The vast surroundings lay open before us. From where we were perched we watched our respective worlds in silence. After a good half hour like this, I ceremoniously helped her to her feet and guided her step-by-step down all nine steps to the street where we stood waiting a bit longer before finding ourselves seated in another black-and-yellow taxi.

The Mumbai heat was becoming oppressive. Whenever the taxi stopped at a red light, we sat in the still heat, sweat streaming down our faces. When the taxi picked up again, we felt the relief of the sea breeze through the open window stinging our skin. Now and then, Rosa Aunty yawned and her head would dangle to the side, drooping more and more until the lurch of the taxi going over a speed bump caused her to wake with a start and straighten herself up.

The outside world seemed alien to me. Our surroundings passed us from the opposite direction with such blinding speed that I wouldn't have been able to recognize the racing geography even if I'd wanted. There were very few Sunday markets open. From the shop signs, I could discern that we had passed Churni Road, the Mahalaxmi neighborhood, and other such places.

I must have dozed off because next thing I knew the driver was informing us we'd reached Mahim Church. Rosa Aunty suddenly became very erect and alert, looking out the window into a maze of lanes cutting across one another. She told the driver to turn down one of them. A narrow lane, the taxi had to maneuver very slowly. Once, twice, several times, Aunty made him turn down other lanes, finally telling him to stop at a four-way intersection.

For a while, she scrutinized the lanes flowing from the intersection, finally deciding on one of them. I held her shaking hand and her bag as she got out of the taxi and clacked excitedly down the lane about fifty paces, then paused.

It was a quiet and ordinary looking lane, like an average street but rife with potholes. Gravel dumps and woodpiles lay scattered throughout. Few doors opened to the lane; rather, most houses were positioned with their backs facing it. At other times of the week, this lane was probably used for parking. Even now there were some cars, covered with a layer of dirt as if they hadn't been moved for years.

She pointed to a tall lamppost that stood by the side of the lane some ten steps away. Reaching it meant squeezing ourselves into the extremely narrow spaces between the burning hot metal parked almost bumper to bumper in the empty lot abutting the lamp. Part of Aunty's frock was coated in a layer of dirt from the metallic bodies. She was breathless in the dusty heat. Yet she moved swiftly and went to stand under the lamppost.

It was a stoic, British-era lamppost with a certain old-world charm and a filigree of ornate motifs so fine that you could gaze at it endlessly and never get tired. The round glass dome was an opaque white. The patch of street below was bathed in the shadow of the adjacent building, thankfully providing us cool, dark shelter. I tried to imagine what sort of glare the lit lamp would throw on the ghostly street at night.

She slid her arms up and down the post, feeling its firm thew. But before long she became still, standing there like a statue, her glazed eyes fixed on a point off in the distance. I was at a loss. There didn't seem to be anything there, at any distance. I stood looking at her, her eyes staring blankly.

It was through my fecund imagination that I saw her. A mirage conjured up by the heat. A youthful hue brimming beneath her pallid skin. Her eyes flickered in the noon sun.

All of a sudden, she stirred, her eyes met mine, and her pallidness returned.

"You are eighteen—" she remarked out of the blue, with the same vague, faraway smile. "Have you ever kissed a girl?"

I could feel the rapid succession of a half-smile, hesitation, embarrassment, and flaming confusion flood my face. I lowered my head and eyes under the weight of her gaze. "No," I mumbled, vigorously shaking my head, "—and I'm fourteen." But I had been kissed before, and I chose to conceal that fact.

After lingering a while longer, we retraced the dusty path. Her hand was limp in mine. Back in the taxi, we slid past a church and, a little farther, stopped at a flower shop. Aunty peeped out the window and asked the driver to honk, whereupon a youth came running from the shop with an enormous bouquet. He wanted to put it on the empty front seat, but Aunty took it and propped it on her small lap. "All seventy-two?" she asked.

"Yes."

"All red roses, no?"

"Yes." His head bobbled from side-to-side.

"Come by later and I'll pay."

"Okay." He made the same head bobbling gesture again.

The taxi lurched into motion. This time the journey wasn't long. In about five minutes we'd reached Old Cadell Road. Aunty took out her diary and, stopping the taxi every few minutes, asked the passersby for the address of one G. M. Kulkarni. It was almost two o'clock in the afternoon when we finally located the place. The sun had peaked, and close by the Arabian sea seethed.

A crowd of twenty-something stood in small clusters in front of the house. Some vehicles were parked on either side of the lane. Aunty didn't hold my hand this time. With one hand she clutched the bouquet to her chest, and with the other she leaned hard on her cane. I carried her bag slung over my shoulder. She asked a gentleman standing nearby, "G. M. Kulkarni . . . ?" and before she could even finish, the gentleman pointed toward the house.

In the veranda lay a body swathed in white sheets. Clumps of incense burned at all four corners of the body, giving off oversweet fumes, and by the head shimmered the bright flame of a large oil lamp, suffused with the scent of grief. Some women were squatted on the ground along the righthand side, while young men bustled in and out of the house, looking busy. They must have been tasked with the preparations for the funeral. In the intensified gloom of the lamp's glare, everyone looked so sorrowful that it was impossible to tell who was family and who an outsider.

It was the dead body of G. M. Kulkarni. The reason we had come here.

To return to the beginning, it had all started that morning soon after sunup, when the neighbor's maid had knocked on our door and shouted to Ma in her high-pitched drawl, "Big Ammi has called you—go quickly." Big Ammi was Rosa Aunty, our neighbor, who in the claustrophobic labyrinth of our neighborhood ran an open-air café where the young crowd came for coffee or a cold drink. Chic English-style umbrellas sheltered small, round tables and chairs. Summers brought a riot of colors to Mumbai and gave the café its special hues—the red, orange, and yellow of wild hibiscus, the pink and purple of queen's crape myrtle, sweet-scented, white spider lilies, and daisies. Apart from the subtle perfume of the flowers, the air was also redolent with the thrilling sweetness of a Chopin nocturne. But inside Rosa Aunty, her inner planted clumps defied growth and atrophied into a stunted thicket of silence. The café—airy, green, and golden—expressed a lifetime of sacrifice and abnegation. She ran the café singlehandedly until her health began to decline, at which point her sister's daughter chipped in to help. Aunty did not wed. She lived alone. With her old maid—who had doddered over to our house asking for Mother. Half an hour later, when Ma returned, I was still in bed, drowsing in the rakish lethargy of my newfound youth. She shook me out of my slumber and said in a matter-of-fact voice, "Some acquaintance of Big Ammi has passed away. You have to accompany her."

"Send Sis," I proposed. "They're both ladies, they'll chat. What will I do? I'll get bored."

"No, no. She asked especially for you. And no one says no to her."

I tossed and turned for some time, rising finally, knowing I'd have to go willy-nilly. Ma came up to me then. "The whole world calls her Big Ammi and today I find out that you call her Rosa?!"

"Not Rosa—Rosa Aunty!" I corrected her, but my voice wavered with all sorts of emotions.

"Yes, yes. Exactly. Rosa. Now get up and get going. And take good care of her."

But I did not tell Ma that I loved that name, Rosa! Or that it had a certain mysterious ring to it that fascinated me. Or that she looked like a heroine from the old, bygone days. Or that I often liked to loll in the café lawn listening to her footsteps winding past each table, the soft murmuring of leaves, the mating call of birds creating a rhythm in the mindless heat.

All of that I hid outright.

This long, hot day, from morning till now, Rosa Aunty and I, we'd been out on our aforesaid mission.

Seventy-two blooms make for an enormous bouquet. So far only a rose or two lay by the deceased; the rest were all marigolds. We removed our footwear outside and approached the body. Everyone turned and looked at us with curiosity as we passed. A woman, about thirty years old, who was draped in white mourning clothes, rose and came to Aunty and inquired with unrecognizing eyes, "You . . . ?"

"Rosemary D'Souza." Aunty responded crisply.

The woman's face remained blank. No one seemed to know Aunty in that gathering. She tried to bend and set down the bouquet, but it was huge and the act threatened to topple her over. I offered her my hand. The woman also offered her hand. And together we three placed the bouquet on the deceased's belly.

It was a good-looking corpse. Shrouded completely in sheets. Only the face was visible. With cotton in the nostrils. This was the first time I'd seen a dead body up close. Aunty was standing—the picture of stillness, the way she'd sat on the library steps—the way she'd stood under the lamppost. Gazing attentively at the deceased's face, hands respectfully clasped, perhaps murmuring a prayer to herself. There was something reverential in her manner that drew people closer, and we all huddled around the deceased, our heads bowed, gazing at his face.

Suddenly it seemed as if the lips of the dead fluttered. We were startled into wakefulness. I looked at Aunty. She was standing, as before, motionless. Wooden. But several of us had seen the corpse's lips flutter momentarily. The lips had parted for a moment, then closed.

The respectful silence of a moment earlier gave way to commotion. People were astounded. They turned to each other, wanting to confirm what they'd just witnessed: Lips moved, right? The dead man's lips fluttered—I saw it, did you?—I did—Me too—Yes, yes, his lips opened and closed—Yes.

A boy hurriedly bent over the body. Removing the cotton from the nostrils, he waved his finger under them, feeling for any breath, any life.

"It looks as if Aaba's lips fluttered. Call the doctor please. Hurry!

Let him check again!" the woman in white cried, with nervous haste. She was his daughter.

A doctor was already there. Swiftly, he placed the end of his stethoscope to the chest, searching for a pulse. Then he waved his finger under the nostrils. He repeated the same examination four or five times. And then he shook his head.

"But his lips moved," insisted the daughter.

The doctor shook his head again.

Despite the doctor's refutation, people still discussed how for a fleeting moment the corpse's lips had fluttered. Slowly the cries of excitement died down. In the arpeggios of the fading chatter, people started leaving. The dead body was ready for its final journey.

Rosa Aunty, who up until then had stood like a statue, stirred. The space left behind by the corpse emptied into her. Her hands, now embracing herself, were just as they'd been earlier, by the lamppost, as if holding a memory open. She took two steps back and, hands folded in namaste, offered a silent gesture of mourning to everyone present, who responded in turn by bringing their palms together.

Then, clutching my hand, Rosa Aunty slowly made her way back outside. It was late evening.

When we'd put a good thirty to forty paces between us and the house, I burst out, my voice high with excitement, "His lips moved. I saw it. I saw it with my own eyes. They moved. I'm dead sure."

"Yes, they moved," said Aunty laconically.

Her eyes were alight with the luster of the brightest constellation in the sky.

"You know," her voice was quiet, "I had faith that he'd come. Maybe just for a moment but he'd come. Even after death he would. Fifty-four years ago, when he was a boy of eighteen, on a street corner under the broken bulb of a lamppost, he left a girl in the middle of a kiss and ran off. She loved him utterly, intensely . . . Today he returned to finish that kiss."

She just stood there, like a princess in a polka-dotted frock. The dazzle of her eyes had now extended to her lips. Everything was dead and silent, as if the roaring sea had suddenly gone still. The fishermen would soon be spreading their nets in its waters, I thought as I watched her tighten her grip on my wrist.

Translator's Note

One day I ask Geet Chaturvedi to write a short story, and he writes it overnight and emails it to me. The story is "The Funeral"—a brave and fascinating story that resounds with a strange longing. The rhythmic clack of the cane, the harsh Mumbai heat, and silence of the space between the real and the surrealist worlds accentuate this effect. I immediately know that I have to translate not just the message but also the movement of language and its strange musicality.

The translation is primarily for the readers of a U.S. journal. As a translator, I have to consider them as I write. So a line such as "Take the money from home" becomes "Come by later and I'll pay." I also rework some of the descriptions into a slightly less formal register that allows the originality of Geet's art to shine through.

My native language is not English, but then English has never been an alien language to Indians. However, I cannot use it as the Americans or the British do. My instinct seems to "cross over to the author" and I let the original's nuances seep into my translation. For instance, when the dialog "All red roses, no?" ends with "no?", it is reflective of the linguistic background (Anglo-Indian) of the character (the elderly Rosa Aunty).

There are conflicts in my pursuit of the closest equivalence, and I make some hard choices. These choices are based on, as J. M. Coetzee puts it, preconceptions, prejudgment, prejudice. The realization that translation can never be the output of an AI language model is a translator's experience.

In a scene in "The Funeral," Rosa Aunty, seated on a step, remarks, "The world we see depends on where we are perched." She makes me think what a privilege it is to look at a creation from my special vantage point called translation.

Settling: Toward an Arabic Translation of the English Word "Home"

Hisham Bustani
translated from the Arabic by Alice Guthrie
The Markaz Review

1

You have no place to retreat to the way defeated armies withdraw into the arms of their soldiers' wives. Nothing casts sheltering shade over you like those archetypal shadow-of-a-man husbands in Egyptian soaps. You don't even have the shade of a wall.

There is no one to lull you into believing that everything is as it should be, no respite in which to restock your anger resources ready for the next day, and no saying that the explosion detonated by the dregs of the night/your scoured-out stamina will be soothed by cold compresses soaked in blossom infusions.

And so you've discovered that you are, in fact, a homeless orphan, a stateless orphan. An uncertain orphan. Lost in the background of the picture, a blurry and cacophonous place. In the foreground are many things that have no real value to you, that mar your transition into a state of full sensory deprivation: walled into white, shrouded in silence. Will my alarm go off now? Will the phone ring? Will the doorbell ring? You teeter on the brink of what will happen, as you think about the last time you saw a moonless sky, a sky full of stars.

The main street is beside the house, cars streaming along it endlessly. A sound like an explosion; red and blue lights reflected on the walls of the buildings; the police raiding a nearby house. You smile to yourself: the door to your apartment is protected by another outer door to which no one but you has a key.

A felled tree, dumped next to a trashcan where cats eat. They creep under just-parked cars at night, drawn to the engines' warmth. You were lopped off from that very tree, since it was so dry and wilted, and the tight space under a car isn't quite suitable for your huge corpse.

You keep on walking.

2

Only when natural semi-disasters happen—snowdrifts, torrential rains that make gushing torrents of the roads—does that rare warmth set in, and that deep silence, and you sleep like a baby.

3

After sipping a little from his cup of coffee, he says: I don't like anyone sharing my bathroom. I don't like for anyone, no matter who they are, to smell the socks I take off after a long day at work. I want my things to be put back exactly where I left them, where they should be. He breaks off, momentarily distracted, then continues: Perhaps . . . perhaps it was a mistake to invite you here. You are doubtless dreaming of kids now, and of us running around after them, and of a weekly grocery list, and a framed family photo on the wall in the hallway. I apologize for involving you, really . . . I can only apologize.

Her eyes widen in astonishment as he gets up to rush out of the café. She has not yet uttered a single word when he draws his coat closed across his belly and hurries away.

4

"Where I lay my head is home."

Try quoting this line to a refugee who begins his journey in Aleppo and does not end up in Germany; a refugee who plunged into the sea and hasn't come back up yet to draw breath; a refugee dying of cold in the forests along the Croatian-Hungarian border.

"Announcement: Hungarian are friendly peoples known for their hospitality, but Hungarian state will take the most stringent measures against anyone who tries to enter its territory illegally. Transiting and crossing the international borders of the Hungarian state illegally is a crime in Hungary and is legal punishing by imprisonment. Do not listen to what the people smugglers tell you! Hungary does not allow migrants to crossing its territory illegally."

Welcome to your new home: fear.

Fear. Fear. Fear. Fear. Those are our four compass points, and fear is our compass itself. There is no homeland for the fearful, and nowhere to settle. For the fearful there are just occasional corners in which to seek sanctuary, to curl up in, to perhaps be missed by that bullet or spared by that glacial night and see one more new morning.

For the fearful there is hope; but hope is delusional, phantasmagoric, and often evaporates, leaving an acrid odor in its wake.

This is why Scheherazade keeps on talking, for her neck is on the line: her homeland is the word. The fugitive keeps moving from one place to another: his homeland is movement. The uneasy keeps constantly questioning: his homeland is doubt. As for the corpse, it found a place to settle down wherever it laid its head: it swooned into a delicious peaceful repose once it stopped searching. It no longer suffers the agony of the breakdown that acceptance brings on.

5

Location: Istiklal Caddesi, Istanbul.

You are drawn to this spot by familiar music and a crowd of people applauding. When you reach it, you discover most of those present are speaking a language you know very well, and singing in it songs of longing for the homeland that they left behind, and dancing: "Take me to my country . . . " Is that what they genuinely wish?

A succession of thoughts slams its way through you now: they would never have sung in the streets of their former cities, if they had done so they would have become prison fodder, been feasted on slowly and leisurely—and now here they are, dancing with wild abandon in the freedom of a coercive homesickness, yearning for a country that tortured them then spat them out onto the open road, left to beg by invoking homelands that take on value only in exile.

You recollect Mahmoud Darwish's definition of longing: "When a sparrow perches on the balcony and seems to be a message from a country you did not love when you were in it as you love it now that it is in you." So you lob a coin into the open guitar case, and get swallowed up by the flood of people moving in every direction.

6

Knock knock knock. You get nervous when people knock on your door. You think no one has the right to wrench you from the warm cuboid womb into which you retreat. You know that the word "warm" here is an exaggeration, because the place is cold in the winter and hot in the summer, it has no capacity—and neither do you, in fact—for moderation.

You will ignore the knocking like you did before, and you will give thanks to every last god and to Mother Nature herself for having illuminated you previously with that genius flash of inspiration that you immediately put into practice by disconnecting the electricity from the doorbell, consigning it to a coma from which it has not yet woken up.

You remember the spiral shape of the shell into which that slimy creature withdraws. You remember the Chinese nested boxes, the Russian matryoshka. "None of you will be able to reach me," thus addressing—at one and the same time—yourself and the person standing on the other side of the door waiting on any sound from inside. Holding your breath, you silently say: *I cannot guarantee a safe outcome.*

Check your permanent fang: When it falls out, you can leave. But it is stable and immobile, and the envelopes are still arriving, with tapes identifying the words:

Today's new words are: sea, motorway, picnic, gun.

The sea: a leather chair with wooden arms, like the one in the lounge. Example: "Don't stay on your feet, sit yourself down on the Sea so we can have a chat."

Motorway: high winds.

Picnic: a very strong and durable material used in flooring. Example: "The chandelier fell to the ground and shattered, but the floor was not damaged because it was made from Picnic."

Gun: a beautiful white bird.

7

Home: a swing with an old rubber tire for a seat. Example: When the boy went to the park with his mother, he insisted on playing on the Home, even though he had fallen out of it the last time they were there.

8

Search log: A tape was found with the specimen that had not arrived inside the usual envelope in the known way. The specimen notes that the tape was found in the roof crawlspace used for storing old, discarded materials. Transcript of the recorded material:

"Home: the place you settle for rather than settling in, but it settles you down." The tape was destroyed under the supervision of the relevant authorities.

9

The time has come to depart.

Notes on Translation

"Where I lay my head is home" is a lyric from "Wherever I May Roam," track five on Metallica's 1991 LP *The Black Album*.

The Hungarian state announcement quoted in section four was published in Arabic in all the Jordanian daily newspapers on September 21, 2015. There were a number of linguistic errors in the original text, reproduced verbatim in the original of this book, and imitated here in the English translation.

"Take me to my country" in section five is a lyric in Fairouz's song "The Wind Whispered to Us" ("nassam alina al-huwa"), words and music composed by the Rahbani brothers.

Mahmoud Darwish's definition of longing in section five is from his book *In the Presence of Absence*, quoted here as translated by Sinan Antoon (Archipelago Books, NY, 2011).

The definitions in italics in section six are taken from the 2009 film *Dogtooth*, directed by Yorgos Lanthimos, in which children who are kept in their parents' home in order to be utterly isolated from the outside world are told that they will be allowed out when their adult canines fall out.

Translator's Note

I translated "Settling: Toward an Arabic translation of the English word 'Home'" as part of *A Last Breath Before it All Ends*, a genre-bending, contemporary Arabic book made up of many wildly heterogenous short and short-short sections. The book contains multitudes, so I was already in the groove of changing voices and styles almost by the page. But perhaps because this particular mini-chapter had originally been commissioned as a standalone piece (for *The Outpost*), it stood out to me as distinct from the rest of the book in a few ways. Central among these was the element of back-translation required to render it into English. There are also intertextuality and cultural references to deal with (not all of them referenced in the original footnotes). The language of the original is oblique yet very precise, the surrealism is not overdone, the political/ethical point being made remains lyrical throughout. All of this made it a satisfyingly difficult piece to get right.

One of the things I enjoy about translating Bustani's work is that he has a combination of qualities I find to be fairly rare in a (cis-male) author: exquisite English proficiency but full trust in the craft of his translators. This means I get to involve him in my process, via long calls or email exchanges over the nano-minutiae of his language, thereby massively enriching my understanding and rendering of his text, whilst knowing I'm in full control of the new piece of art I'm creating in English. In other words, my creative and intellectual labor is fully valued. This is, of course, not always the case for translators. Hisham's day job as a dental surgeon also means I get a second opinion on my dental x-rays—no small matter for us Brits, famous for having some of the worst dentists in the world.

The Lion

Farhad Pirbal
Translated from the Kurdish by Jiyar Homer and
   Alana Marie Levinson-LaBrosse
Your Impossible Voice

Standing at the window of his room, a chill breeze tousling his hair, he spared a glance for the snow piling up on the sill and sighed, "That's it then. This is my life now: always this cold and wretched wandering from this little room to the rooftop and from the rooftop back inside, like a prisoner." Other refugees, people he considered friends, from Sri Lanka, Chile, Iran, and Lebanon, who had lived isolated out here for months before he even arrived, told him it could be nearly a year living like this on the island; after that, God only knows which far-flung city of this arctic country they might dispatch him to.

Just then, he heard a ship's whistle: little by little, until it came into view from his window, the ship edged away from the island's shore. It was their island's ferry, leaving, like every other evening, loaded with refugees headed to Copenhagen (Copenhagen!), another cold and empty island. And just what would he do if he went to Copenhagen? Who would he see?

Standing at his room's window, he watched the ship splashing and spuming away, little by little drawing away from their shore. Irritable, currycombing his own heart, he muttered, "Really. So what if I go to Copenhagen? What can I do there? Who do I know? Who knows me?"

Just a few days ago, he'd had this gut feeling, "You shouldn't just sit in this room. Come on. You should get away from this island for a

little while, like everyone else. If nothing else, go get some fresh air."
So, with other refugees, from Lebanon, Sri Lanka, and Poland, he got
on the ship and went to Copenhagen.

The ship docked at Copenhagen's Vesterport at three thirty in the
afternoon. As he disembarked, he calculated that he had, like every
other refugee, until six thirty in the evening (so three hours) until he
must be waiting again at the port: to catch the boat and return to his
island to eat dinner and sleep.

When he reached Copenhagen's bazaar, at four o'clock in the
afternoon, he had no idea where to go or what to do. He searched
and sauntered down the city center's streets, same as his first visit to
Copenhagen's bazaar, same as his second visit, same as his third, same
as every time he'd come: lonely, no cash, no currency, a stranger, a
wandering child, his eyes searching the stores and their colorful dis-
plays, his glance lingering on the golden six- and eleven-story apart-
ment buildings. Eager, thirsty, when he could, he loosed the sling of
his glance at the reddish-blonde, silken-haired girls. And when he
tired, he sat down on a cold garden bench. Rested, he stood to walk
once more, eyes roving, exploring until he exhausted himself once
again. And in the end, when he made it back to the walking district
along the shore, to Vesterport, he felt a fatal strangeness and solitude.
A strangeness and solitude that gnawed noisily on his innermost soul.
And back on the ship, on the way back to the island, he heard the ref-
ugees, some in broken English, others in Persian and Arabic, insulting
the Danish people, spitting on Denmark's weather. One of the Iranian
refugees, who seemed more educated than all of them, turned to a
Lebanese refugee and said in English, "Ibn Battuta, on page 285 of his
travel journal, wrote: 'Denmark has foul language, foul weather, and
foul manners.'"

The raucous, foul-mouthed refugees filled him with disgust; not
even back in the island's cramped dining hall, not even mid-bite, did
they leave off from their fighting, rioting, and insulting. So strange. So,

really, why had Miss Anneli, the supervisor of the island's refugees, commented the other night, "You have a lovely name"? So strange. Miss Anneli, as soon as they met, with her lovely smile, had drawn closer to him to ask, "What's your name?"

He had said, "Sherzad."

Miss Anneli, always curious, then asked, "Sherzad . . . and does that mean anything in Kurdish?"

"Yes."

"And what meaning is that?"

"A lionhearted man."

I still don't get it. That woman, why did she say, "You have a lovely name"? Was she just trying to show a refugee kindness? Yes, perhaps, so that if nothing else, for a moment or two, the clouds of the disquiet and foreignness he felt would clear.

Miss Anneli, before the evening she commented on his name, had glanced at him a few times with growing curiosity. The first time, he had stood alone on the beach, leaning against an old shipwreck, dispirited, despondent, gazing at the far-flung horizon of the Baltic Sea, his eyes brimming with foreignness. Suddenly, Miss Anneli brushed past him, taking in his sorrow-wracked posture with eyes that held questions, compassion, and mercy. The second time, he was on the building's rooftop, once again on his own, a thick, black coat draped over his shoulders. He sat on some piled gravel, huddled against the cold, head bowed as he contemplated a feeble, bony chicken pecking the ground beside the gravel, searching for worms or grain. Just then, Miss Anneli passed by with a sisterly glance full of compassion and the most lovely smile. Yes, it all comes down to this: people in various states of loneliness and brokenness and misery getting pitied by others.

Agh! Poor Sherzad! Twenty-nine years! Twenty-nine years full of comfort, courage, and love, twenty-nine years he had lived, full of delight and pride . . . and so, that's, well, that's that . . . today, on this far-flung island, far from his country, far from his childhood, far from the paradise of his youth, miserable, he weeps over his solitude and brokenness! Agh! A sigh of remorse escaped him as he hung his head and left the window to sit at the table in the middle of the room.

There was a small mirror on the table, propped up next to an apple and a slice of grilled chicken. Today, in the dining hall at lunch, as at every other meal, he couldn't help but be disgusted by the refugees' constant riot. A Lebanese refugee at the table picked a fight with a Sri Lankan refugee. They fell on each other, a riot broke out, and though he knew he couldn't finish his salad, he packed his slice of grilled chicken and his apple in Saran Wrap, put them in a bag, and got up. He took them back to his room and put them on the table.

Sitting, silent, he stared at the slice of chicken and the apple in front of him. Suddenly, he grinned.

Suddenly, he was a kid again! He saw himself clearly walking through their orchard with his mother. A naughty boy, as he walked, he kicked the apples that had fallen, whatever his feet could reach. His mother scolded him tenderly, "Sherzad, my boy, this is a sin! Stop kicking the apples!"

And here, now, today, after all those many years, on this arctic island in the middle of nowhere, his daily lunch is always a slice of chicken and just one single apple! Just a single apple!

He planted his elbows on the table. His claws, this side and that, clutched at his skull. As he looked back, a sob caught in his throat. He raised his head and looked at himself in the small mirror on the table: a tangle of hair, a fistful of beard, two thick, drooping eyebrows slowly growing together . . . and his eyes, so strange! Each day more sunken.

So strange! This evening, in front of the mirror, with his disheveled appearance and his withered soul, he looked exactly like the mournful, broken lion he had seen in his village nineteen years before! Now, he remembers it as if it were a dream. One evening, he was at home with his mother, aunt, sisters, and brothers, eating near the hearth, when a lion, a long rope trailing after him, crept into their courtyard to collapse on the porch.

His little sister's eyes, when they lit on the lion, flew open wide. She leveled a finger, pointing outside, and screamed, "Lion!"

It was the first time in their lives they'd seen such a wonder: late one evening, a lion creeps into their courtyard to collapse on their porch! And with their father for years gone on a journey he'd yet to return from.

His mother, when her eyes lit on the lion, sprang to her feet; she attacked the door handle, slammed the door shut, and threw the dead-bolt. Then, together, they all rushed to the window. He, his mother, his aunt, and his younger siblings piled on top of each other, in a tangle of questions, fears, and exclamations, each trying to get a glimpse of the lion. And the lion, exhausted, spent, and whimpering, just lay against the porch walls. In the moonlight, his muddled, dirty mane managed to shine. Blood leaked from his forehead and both temples and from his skull, down around his ears, viscous anguish drip, drip, dripped.

How strange! It seemed the lion had come from a long way off and saw their porch as a peaceful shelter where he could rest a while. Perhaps he had been driven away by others. From time to time, with his bloody mane, he shook himself. He chafed feebly against his rope, his limbs shaking, but couldn't rid himself of it.

Agh! Now, here, on this island, Sherzad imagines himself as the lion of his childhood. Agh! In his entire life, he had never seen himself so miserable, alone, and broken. His aunt, he remembers, had pressed herself up against the glass, nearly putting herself through it, to see the lion. She said, "This lion . . . must be, war broke him."

His mother, as if begging for mercy, said, "A lion so dispirited and powerless? So faint? So miserable? Let me see no more."

His little brother, all in a rush, asked his mother, "What is that long rope wrapped around his neck?"

And his little sister, whose fear hadn't yet faded, said, "Mother . . . he must have escaped some prison."

For nearly half an hour, they stood beside the window and contemplated the lion. And the lion on the porch stayed sprawled in the same spot; he didn't dare—he couldn't even—lift his head to look around. From time to time, he waved his hands weakly around his head, trying to shoo away the flies that had settled on the bloody wounds at his temples—and even at that, he sometimes failed, flies still buzzing around his head and swarming his wounds. From time to time, he changed flanks, settling down once more with a wounded sigh.

In the end, his mother could no longer bear the sight; she stood with sudden resolve and said, "I am going to give him meat."

His aunt protested; she did not approve. His younger siblings, feeling the same, gathered around their mother, climbed into her lap and shouted, "No, for God's sake, don't go!"

His mother said, "Enough." She bundled up a slice of grilled chicken from last night's leftovers and an apple in some Saran Wrap and opened the door. "I'll just go put it in front of him," she said.

His younger siblings and aunt, all together, silent and wide-eyed, watched their mother from the window as slowly, so slowly, with hesitant steps, she approached the lion. And the lion lay still against the porch wall.

A terrible silence, springing from fear, disquiet, and shock, took hold of them all. Through the window, they saw: their mother stood before the lion, holding out the Saran-wrapped apple and slice of chicken. Then, steadily, she bowed and placed the apple and slice of chicken on the ground.

They couldn't believe their own eyes. Open-mouthed, agitated, in shock, they waited impatiently for their mother to come back to safety, when they could let loose their happiness and riot and laugh.

Suddenly, a strange laugh, almost a roar, rose from the window.

He started, as if returning to consciousness from an otherworldly dream; tired and weak, he raised his head to look at the apple and slice of chicken before him, feeling fatal misgivings and misery, sorrow about to shatter him.

Mitte Grand Island – 1985

Translators' Note

We came to "The Lion" from dramatically different ends of the spectrum as translators. Jiyar had primarily translated prose at that point, while Alana had primarily translated poetry. Jiyar was dedicated to the immediate legibility and colloquial feel of English and Alana was interested in the images, often drawn from the body, that Kurds build their language from. Both of us knew each other well. We knew that collaborating would challenge our inclinations as translators. We imagined that the tension between our approaches could serve an author like Farhad Pirbal well, particularly in a story like "The Lion" that straddles contradictions: the concrete and abstract, the real and unreal, the "us" and "other," the human and animal bodies. One could argue that "The Lion" addresses the inhumanity of displacement and the false piety of pity, and one could argue with equal validity that the story exists in the singular image of the lion. One can argue and, oh, have we argued. Describing our reasoning for each minute decision we might make took persistence. We never moved on from a decision without reaching understanding and agreement. At times, we grew impatient, but that is the nature of understanding: it does not arrive on schedule. Sometimes, it makes us wait. Sometimes, we wait so long we begin to unravel. Then, there it is, wandering into the courtyard, mangy and broken and unbelievable.

Joyful Mythology

Zuzanna Ginczanka
translated from the Polish by Joanna Trzeciak Huss
The Hopkins Review

Like Atlas, on my shoulders I proudly carry my own sky—
I stretch upward like:
nitrogen—
oxygen—
steam—
the barometer of my heart presses blood like quicksilver
to measure the weight of happiness
on the scale of the pulse of speech;

but I don't know the digits that compasses read
and I don't know the numbers for barometric pressure
when at night the heavy heavens
in the limbs
of my
arms
bloom with the brilliance of stars like the fine blossoms
of cherries—
This is quite the trick:
to bear your own happiness—
joyfully,
sacrilegiously
unbowed by heaven—
Like Atlas, on my shoulders I proudly carry a dark blue space,

where the copper sun
marks
its course
in buttercups.—

January 1, 1934

Translator's Note

"Joyful Mythology" (Mitologia radosna), written when Ginczanka was sixteen years old, relies on an imaginative embodiment of the plight of Atlas, and a physical universalizing of it. Here she casts herself in a role that had traditionally been the province of the masculine. My task was to capture her careful blending of two strains of the Atlas myth: the Greek, in which Atlas is condemned by Zeus to bear the weight of the heavens on his shoulders, and the Roman, recounted in Ovid's *Metamorphoses*, where Perseus turns Atlas into a mountain range, with his hair becoming a forest. Taken together, this yields the image of Mount Atlas bearing the weight of the heavens. In this respect, Ginczanka can be seen as universalizing the plight of Atlas, not only extending it to herself, carrying her own sky on her shoulders, but to all of us: through the phenomenon of barometric pressure, we all bear the weight of the sky (an insight shared with me by my colleague, classicist Jennifer Larson). The multivalent word *niebo* (sky/heaven/the heavens), a word whose weight is never easy to bear, led me to lean on all three possibilities, as I sensed a shift from the physical to the metaphysical and back again. An important part of the translation process is tracking down not only elements of mythology, but also of botany. In the poem's final stanza, Ginczanka references *jaskier*, which broadly refers to flowers of the genus *Ranunculus*. This is a large genus that includes crowfoots, spearworts, and buttercups. This poses not only the problem of what Ginczanka had in mind, but also what would make poetic sense in the translation. In this case it amounts to deciding what the last word of the poem will be: crowfeet? crowfoots? spearworts? No. Buttercups.

[This page holds the place of a piece withdrawn from the anthology by its author. It honors and offers respect to those who suffer, bear witness, and bring testimony in whatever ways their conscience and circumstances permit, and holds our gratitude also to their translators, both present and absent from these pages.]

The Snail's Spiral

Disney Cardoso (in collaboration with
    Christian Rincón)
translated from the Spanish by Jeanine Legato
Consequence

I met Gato six months after joining the guerrilla. We saw each other
for the first time in La Llaneta, a rural settlement near Marquetalia.
We were attending a training for new recruits and he and I were cov-
ered in mud from head to toe. We couldn't stop looking at each other,
intuiting a certain complicity or maybe the common solitude of those
of us who arrive young to the guerrilla. The afternoon drawing to a
close, we went for a swim in one of the nearby rivers. We began talking
as the water cleansed our faces, and right then we knew we would be
friends. We were fifteen years old and laughed uncontrollably as we
tore through the landscape that, through play, revealed itself to us.

•

One afternoon as we were making chontos—latrines dug in the earth
in the middle of the jungle—we saw the snails for the first time. They
were as big as coins and their shells had spirals that slowly receded
before culminating in a center beyond view. Gato and I looked at each
other, began gathering them in our hands, and tossed them at one
another. Chucking and ducking, laughing, lobbing them again. At that
moment, Gato came up with the game with which we would horse
around on so many days that followed this one. It was simple: we
traced a square in the earth and put various snails in it. I held another

snail in my hand, stroking it with my fingertips, warming it in my grip, and then threw it at the square so it would collide there with another. One life against another. The one who managed to break one of the shells within the square won, breaking the spiral.

•

I had attempted suicide five times. That was before joining the guerrilla. It's just that so many things went on in my house. My sister didn't love me, for example, and when my mom left with her partner for weeks on end, she would take control and throw me out of the house. On those days I had to sleep up in a mango tree. The nights, the days, the water, the heat—it's incredible how a neglected person adapts to any situation. For this reason, when the guerrilla passed by my house, I went running after them so they would take me. The commander leading the unit said that I was too young, but I insisted that I was already fifteen, that I would never regret having gone. I told them about everything going on in my house, the days and nights, and they finally agreed. I didn't want to look back.

•

Today, I can still remember Gato in great detail. I squint my eyes and see him beside me: he had light hair and green eyes framed by abundant lashes. I remember his many freckles and his nose that sloped into a small nub capable of predicting flare-ups in the weather. His sister who, for practical reasons, we called Gata, was much shorter than he and wore her hair shoulder length. They both shared those freckles and the trenches, and it was odd not to see them together at any hour of the day. She had protruding canine teeth, which is perhaps why she hardly smiled. Gato, on the other hand, would laugh at the slightest opportunity. I can remember him, snail in hand, and his nervous gaze when we were before the commander.

"Comrade Betty! You two know that you can't go on behaving like children."

"Comrade Betty, you're disruptive!"

"Comrade Betty acts like a child."

"You are a young woman, Betty, not a kid. Betty, you are a *se-ño-ri-ta*."

"It turns out we have some disorderly comrades. Take a step forward, comrade Betty."

And I would step forward.

"What is it you need? Do you two want me to get you dolls so you can behave? Why are you acting like this?"

"You two need to bring some order to your lives. I'm going to read you the code again."

They read us the code over and over again. After we repeated it aloud, they punished us with gathering the firewood or guarding the animal traps. Gato would look at me, stifling his laughter.

•

Those years were cloaked in unexpected happiness, thanks to the snails. I had them in my pockets, my hands, I stuck them to tree bark during the night and the next day retrieved them from slightly higher on their slow escape, restarting the game.

The first time I went to the shooting range and saw the circles closing around the target, I thought again of the snail, and the shot fired straight. To grow is to retreat from the center and move outward.

•

That first year in the FARC was really tough. I thought of my mom constantly, even though she was never around and had never helped me when I needed her most. I cried every night because, one way or another, I was beginning to miss everything from which I'd escaped. I tried not to make noise and dried my tears as soon as they fell, but my memory was open-ended, filling me with illusions and deceptions. Cast it off, avoid it, laugh, cry, cast it off again.

•

I remember they gave us sweets or cigarettes on Tuesdays and Wednesdays. Since I didn't smoke, I chose sweets which I used afterwards to make bets with Gato. Every once in a while other kids filled out our group, but we generally ended up playing just the three of us. So many times were we publicly or secretly called out and punished that the rest preferred to keep their distance. They were afraid of the penance the commanders so often assigned us, so Gato, his sister, and I became a spiral that closed in on itself.

•

The nature that surrounded me was cold with lush, grand trees. I had learned how to distinguish many kinds of green and to remember some of the names of the trees from those long expeditions we took: guamo, cucharo, guásimo, arrayán, bejucos. When we finished our chores, and sometimes sooner, we climbed up and balanced ourselves in the crown of the trees to experience fear. We were rabidly happy and didn't care about falling because it was going to happen to us anyway in the war, and we were better off if it happened due to a decision rather than by accident. Rehearse the mistake. I recall entwining the branches to walk between trees; I recall a heavy Gato, lowering himself from a treetop, and Gata climbing in a hurry. One of those many times, it so happened that Gata couldn't hold herself up well and the weight of the tree sent her flying into a mulberry bush. Its small thorns had embedded themselves in her face and legs, and she nearly fainted while we removed them. Gato and I laughed with panic.

•

I knew that my sister had also joined the guerrilla a little while after I had left. I was in the 21st Front and she in the Daniel Aldana Bloc. We didn't see each other for twenty-two years. Every so often we received vague news, one about the other, but it wasn't until the peace process was finalized that we met again. When we saw each other, we hugged as if by instinct, and we agreed that we had survived for so long because of our mother's prayers, words that care, conceal, grasp. That long journey had ended. We would go home again. Gato and Gata ended up in the guerrilla because they were left parentless. Their parents were well known for their practice of black magic. When the guerrilla snatched the books on witchcraft with which they had worked, Gato secretly held on to one. For a year he carried it hidden in the seat of his underwear or in his boots, until one day, led by who knows what desire, he wanted to cast a spell. He decided to gather the hearts of three black hens, three hearts of swallows, and other exotic elements. He, as well as I, knew that this type of thing wasn't allowed. When our comrades grew suspicious and found the book, they burned it before his eyes. Amidst his rage and grief, Gato was harshly sentenced to fetch firewood two hundred fifty times. I asked to go with him to soften his punishment and, on one of these trips, dropping the wood to the ground, he said:

"Let's leave, Betty. Gata and I are going to leave."

"No, I can't. I still have a lot to lose."

"I know you won't tell anyone."

I shook my head, grabbed the wood that had been dropped, and turned my back to them, knowing that I would never see them again.

Hours later, the others went looking for them, but they were too far ahead. From the others, I learned that they had confronted their old comrades with rifles that same night to save their lives and that, after a long battle, they had escaped unharmed.

•

My nom de guerre was Betty and the name given to me by my mom is Pabliny. So as not to forget this transition, I carried a notebook in which I wrote everything that happened to me. I haven't forgotten how, twenty days after arriving, Gato gave me a notepad that drowned soon after. The river took longer carrying it away than I did in looking for another because, one way or another, I always found a way to put my thoughts on paper.

"Why do you write down that nonsense?" Gato would ask me.

"So that I don't forget it."

"You must be crazy if you can't remember."

But what I carried in those notebooks wasn't my memory but my heart, which is another way of going back and moving forward. I remember that I often had to write in secret on sheets of paper I saved in baggies so they wouldn't get wet when I crossed rivers and streams. I had even made a new pocket in my pack so they wouldn't find anything during inspections.

The last notebook I got, one that I still have, I got through Guzmán, who was my partner during many years and who was in charge of distributing supplies to us. He would ask me to help him keep a record of the things doled out, and I took advantage and asked him to bring me more notebooks.

One day he asked me about it, and I told him that they had gotten wet. He never mentioned it again even if in the end he knew what I was doing. Every page was an imprint, a scene unfinished in my eyes that survived by my hand, by writing it, by commenting on it, so that every page of the notebook had a different title: Tatiana, Kisses, Clouds, Between Branches, Names of Flowers, Espeletia Genus.

•

"Comrade Betty, playing with snails again?"

•

The struggle was something I also waged within. Alone, within myself. I feel the breeze come down from the mountain and I think I, too, am this drizzle that cleans my face, I am this AK-47 to which I cling effortlessly because the years have gone by, and I am also on the other side of the gunfire, but I am also here. I am a tree that seemingly does not move but tells its story undaunted from beneath the soil. It is my way of arriving home more quickly, of telling my mother that I am on my way, to heal my hands, to kiss my forehead, to tell me that I am not so alone and to forgive each other the silence of having answered to different names. Conquer or die, goes the battle cry. Conquer dying, I say. I am already here, farther still.

Translator's Note

In 2020, four years after the Final Agreement to End the Armed Conflict and Build a Stable and Lasting Peace was signed by the Colombian government and the Revolutionary Armed Forces of Colombia (FARC-EP), something remarkable took place: a group of demobilized combatants, in collaboration with the Master's in Creative Writing at the Instituto Caro y Cuervo and the Center for Memory, Peace, & Reconciliation, undertook a collective writing process resulting in the publication of *Naturaleza común: relatos de no ficción de excombatientes para la reconciliación*.

The concept that united the writers featured in the collection was the environment itself and how, in the words of Juan Álvarez, project coordinator, it had "been a victim, but also, paradoxically, a beneficiary of the armed conflict." This piece, "The Snail's Spiral," was written by one of the eleven cosigners of the peace agreement who participated in the writing process.

This offering by Disney Cardoso, in collaboration with Christian Rincón and translated by me, highlights the importance of process on multiple levels, not the least of which is the level of Colombian peacebuilding, at once roiled by setbacks, yet upheld by people like Cardoso whose apuesta para la paz (a bid—a gamble?—for peace) is steadfast against unimaginable odds (such as the ongoing assassination, by the hundreds, of ex-combatants who have returned to civilian life).

Beyond the circumstances in which this text emerged, I think Cardoso's beautiful exploration of betwixt and betweenness (and the writing process) will, on another level, resonate with translators. For it is in translation that we play with and "rehearse the mistake" of language transference, note—like Cardoso—the grief and gain of calling things by their different names, and build something new with the words in transition in our notebooks that can survive by our hand, or be lost to the river.

To Disney and Juan for the opportunity to add another layer to this collective construction—thank you.

Water_Miniatures: Unboxing

Gala Pushkarenko
translated from the Russian by Dmitri Manin
AzonaL

1.

Object: It seems to me important to know that we can't speak
It seems to me important to realize that you can't say: snow

Unboxing: White drowning in itself. A face of a face. A catch.
Warmth consists of shifted wind, right?
Cold consists of shifted sense, right?
To break down a half-answer.

There's no such question really

2.

Object: like you touch the wallpaper with your hand and the
        wall isn't there
Should you poke it through?

Unboxing: There's always someone who gets drunk at the party
Today it's me
He still can't imagine that it's possible to
fall out of love with him
I was taught how to live with PTSD, and they weren't
I used to hate myself just as you are hating me now

So what did this actor_ine do here?
She acted out how people die in movies

Clearly: this is when it's not facts that you know but the witness'
     story

The enclosed liquid
has been formatted

3.

Object: I think I have to admit: to observe dthth is mesmerizing
     (a mesmerizing childhood)
Unboxing: You were a good cat I love you

4.

Object: It seems to me important to know that we can't speak
It seems to me important to realize that you can't say: revolution

Unboxing: if you don't wash the knife the pineapple
tastes like meat

Pineapple (looking at a chocolate bar but not eating):
it's imperative to go down the subway at once
: to cross

Meat: concurrently body

Knife: walking the gallery
: rechristened acmeism as dismembered loneliness

5.

Object: I think I have to admit that
I love Russian poetry

Unboxing: in '83 in Leningrad
he swore he'd show me the Louvre
(I was a-fucki@ng-mazed)

I want to gift you a scene
(a mask)
when I run between pregnant horses
That's a whole lot of images in one line
: a demarche has to be
a plaything

(to see how you cut open the run)

6.

Object: I think I have to admit that
I don't like Russian literature

Unboxing: I want ice cream (that's between the lines)

Plus two paths need to be connected
<you have a strange photo in your wallet:
your wife giving birth: taken from the side as you
stroke her still-pregnant belly>

and

<I feel uneasy when

I can't picture someone I'm on the phone with at the moment>

(and now he's eating me and I'm nearly coming)

Yes, what I'm doing is politics:
I'm screwed into freedom
We are screwed into the freedom of the thread
of the flights of stairs
to contain the upper and lower approaches to the window
which support
and balance
the flat planes of our dreams

Their voids keep the house speedy

Translator's Note

My Facebook feed is full of Russian poetry shared by poets in real time. Since Russia invaded Ukraine, it's all wartime work: words of grief, defiance, disbelief, vengeance. But it was still before the war that I first encountered the work of Gala Pushkarenko, started following the poet's posts, and soon saw a poem that I felt I had to translate. It intrigued me, and I wanted to get to know it more closely and to share it.

"Water_Miniatures" defies common classifications and oppositions. It's both intellectual and sensual, free-flowing and rigidly structured, in a sense it's even long and short at the same time. The poem's overarching theme, to me, is the nature of meaning and representation. Consider this line, for example: "She acted out how people die in movies"—this act is removed by two degrees of signification from an actual death. I read "boxing" and "unboxing" as metaphors of writing and reading. But the poem is far from being that straightforward. It admits multiple interpretations and doesn't give answers—rather, it poses questions and makes you think them over. Of course, I tried to keep my translation as ambiguous and fluid as the original text with its potential for multiple interpretations.

After this first translation, I've been translating the poet's new work, now dominated by traumatic wartime experiences and difficult reflections. You can find it here: http://articulationproject.net/15347.

A Body

Catalina Infante Beovic
translated from the Spanish by Michelle Mirabella
Columbia Journal

We found a body in the bathroom. It wasn't wearing any underwear; it wasn't wearing any clothing at all. The body was wet, face down; its arm was twisted, with the palm of its hand toward the ceiling. We could hear the shower running from the moment we entered the bedroom, or maybe even before that, from the moment we opened the apartment door using the key the building super kept on hand for emergencies. Maybe that body was in the habit of showering with the door open. Maybe it didn't manage to close the door, or it wanted to leave the water running while walking around naked. Who knows. Here I could skip to the part where later, in the hospital, they told us that the body had high blood pressure, that it had suffered a heart attack, which could have been avoided if it had taken care of itself. But some memories surfaced between the bathroom and the hospital that I don't want to gloss over.

Neither of us cried when we saw it. My sister just took the body and, struggling, turned it over. She laid it on the floor on its back. Its eyes were closed, and its brow was split open. My sister rested the head in her lap and sat on the wet floor. She took her phone out of her backpack, dialed a number, deleted it, then dialed another. Who knows who she was trying to reach as I looked at the split-open brow of a face I could hardly recognize. I looked at that large, white body, the scars on its stomach. I wondered if that body was dead, if it would fall to us to dress it, to put on the makeup. I wondered if it had any suits, because bodies wear suits when they're placed in coffins. I wondered if bodies found like this had to be taken to the hospital, if that's what was done. Or if we could simply put it in the car and bring it to the police or a funeral home—the only one I know of came to mind, a vague image of a half-lit neon sign, on the corner of Bustamante or Vicuña Mackenna. I used to mix those two streets up when I was a girl.

I got in touch with Susana and asked her to call an ambulance, my sister said. I didn't want to ask her why she didn't just call an ambulance herself, because I wouldn't know how to call one either, which number to dial. I also wouldn't know where to tell them to go, whether to the hospital, a funeral home, Susana's house. I also wouldn't know how to explain the body, why it was there, sprawled out on a bathroom floor. I couldn't even say if it was dead or not.

Here I could skip this part and jump to when later we were in the waiting area at Salvador Hospital hoping that a doctor would speak with us. I could talk about how the emergency room was flooded due to a clogged toilet, and that the pee smell connected us with a state more profound than any silence, fear, or introspection. I could continue the story from there, it would be easier, but there were other memories in that bathroom, scenes my sister and I had blocked out. She kept her gaze locked on her phone; she didn't want to look me in the eye, stiff before an unclothed body that I hadn't seen in over fifteen years, and that she had visited behind my back these past few weeks. We were reminded then of a scene, both of us at the same time. We didn't just look alike physically to the point of confusion, we also thought in the same way, felt nearly the same way, had the same memories. Or at least that's what I believed. In that memory the two of us are there, many years ago, in a car with our matching pajamas, as that body drives slowly down Vicuña Mackenna or Bustamante. The lights from the signs stream through our eyelids, painting our faces in shades of red, blue, and orange.

Here I could pull us out of that bathroom and jump right into describing our hermetic mouths, standing in a corner of that room which reeked of pee. But other memories came, before the building super and some neighbors showed up; before the paramedics struggled to lift the body onto the stretcher and then into the ambulance; before arriving at Salvador Hospital; and before an aspiring doctor, no older than twenty-seven, told us, in the middle of the night, that the body had suffered a heart attack. As my sister stared at her phone, we were reminded of that scene in silence. I don't know how or in what order the scene must've come to my sister's mind, but in mine, I recalled how that body pulled open our covers in the middle of the night. How it secretly put us in the car. How it drove slowly down that street full of lights. How it parked in a small alleyway, outside Susana's house. How we feigned sleep, afraid to open our eyes, terrified to talk to each other, pretending to fall into a deep sleep until we actually did. The next day we woke up at Susana's, asking no questions, because we children didn't ask questions. Over the years we accepted that night as a dream that we never spoke of. And while I observed that body whose face I hardly remembered, my sister didn't cry, but she did tell me that this body had contacted her a few weeks ago, that it wanted to see the two of us, that that night should've been so different. That that afternoon she and the body talked about some trivial topics along with others that were a bit confusing. That it had asked her for us to forgive it, for abandoning us like that, that it wanted so much to see the two of us. You can't forgive a body you hardly know, I said to my sister. Then she did cry, as if she were saying goodbye. I tried to do it too, the crying. But I couldn't.

So here's where I can now tell the part about how they took the body to an operating room, that we waited suspended in the pee smell of that place, that my sister's clothes were stained and I remained stiff among the people. That after a few hours the doctor came out and explained to us that it had been a heart attack, that it could've been avoided if it had cared for itself, that the only thing left to do was to contact a funeral home, that they had the information for one nearby, on Bustamante or Vicuña Mackenna.

Translator's Note

"A Body" is the fifth story in Chilean author Catalina Infante Beovic's story collection *Todas somos una misma sombra* (Neón Ediciones, 2018). The source text is written in Spanish, a null-subject language, allowing Infante Beovic to deliberately leave the story bereft of subject pronouns when referring to the body for which the story is named. In doing so, she makes use of Spanish grammar to emphasize the narrator's emotional detachment from the person, whatever gender, who once inhabited that body. Accounting for this in English, a non-null-subject language, presented a translation challenge. To create that sense of detachment in the English, where the Spanish had no explicit subject in reference to the body, I chose to use the pronoun "it" or to insert "the body." Where the Spanish uses absence, the English pronoun "it" works to objectify, thereby depersonifying the body and transforming it into an object for dispassionate observation through the narrator's eyes. This intentional choice in the Spanish, reflected in the English translation, not only creates a sense of emotional detachment but also obscures any material information about the body and its relationship to the narrator. As the story unfolds, the narrative provides context that gradually allows the reader to fill in what is conspicuously absent.

From *Unstill Life with Cat*

Anna Felder
translated from the Italian by Brian Robert Moore
Asymptote

CHAPTER ONE

They took me for a cat because I played my part well. Another was a purple grape, or an old man, a lady blackbird. I was a cat.

I'd open my eyes and see before me a whole apple, which was all I needed to fall back asleep; it was just the two of us, me and the apple, and it was only right. I'd close my eyes, and if I opened them again it was purely out of scrupulousness, to say "sure is an apple"—sometimes it's nice to put yourself to the test, to clear up that doubt that you didn't have. Later you go forward with your eyes closed, it's the scent of apple that you smell from up close, from two centimeters away but you're already in it by now, underneath the taut skin; the apple stays smooth and whole and green, only it's been flattened with snout on top of paws, and the juice inside turns warm and heavy enough for you to feel it throbbing.

They were sleeps laid out on horizontal surfaces. Without moving, the surfaces replaced each other, one by one, tables which must have been made of plastic or wood, a baby's changing table, an ironing board, getting larger and more immaterial over time, but always horizontal, and vast, similar to certain views from above, when in the evening above the rooftops you don't lift or lower your head, but keep square in your pupils the darkening line of the horizon.

The voices, if there were any, or the braking of a car at a turn, were stretched into razor-thin threads inside us, were flattened into the slightest sheets of metal foil that glisten in the light.

You went from one season to the next without even moving, feeling the approaching damp, the scent of apples, and the winter was almost in us, another one of those surfaces stretched on the ground, advancing while we stayed still, even the flowerbeds keeping motionless under the broken branches. You could listen to the chill coming, the old man felt it in his hands, he complained as he showed the chilblain in his frozen mitts.

"Life of the old," he said. "Now it's their turn," and with his hand he'd gesture out there, but they weren't always out and about.

"We did our part," he repeated two or three times. "We put in our years."

He didn't turn around to speak; he looked straight in front of him the way old people do: it's their way of looking back.

I listened to him the way I'd listen to the radio: I'd stay close to it, a box twice as wide as the old man, which, when it spoke, made the voice of the announcer or of the singing lesson; I'd take anything—the woman's hour, Nabucco—and I'd doze off, they were quiet hours to pass in some way; I wouldn't have missed a single word for anything in the world, I'd even take the old man's cough if he was the one speaking. If he stayed quiet, he was a mute radio, which kept company all the same.

CHAPTER THREE

I was an impartial cat: if they called me, I'd come, whether it was the old man or someone else, so long as there was a reason. Or else I'd wait for them to come to me. I'd wait and say, "Let's wait and see."

The announcer called out to check if they were home: if Nabucco or his wife were home, then she could avoid going downstairs. She called out again, shouting, "No one's home"—but she didn't get an answer. Then she came down the two flights of stairs and went straight into the kitchen: the coffeepot was ready on the stove, she only needed to light it and wait. She filled my bowl too, lukewarm water mixed with milk, but I didn't find it enticing—milk at that time of day does nothing for me. She didn't insist, but looked around the kitchen; she took one of the singing teacher's shoes and slipped it onto her foot: it was a little big on her, but you could tell that she liked the model, she looked at herself straight on and from the side to be totally convinced. I could only judge from behind; I was sitting in the old man's spot, waiting for the announcer to turn around: I determined that to switch off the flame under the coffee she'd have no choice but to turn. Now she had picked up both shoes and was twisting them between her fingers to make sure it was good leather; I can't say if she still found them to her liking, she might have and she might not have: the announcer was the only person in the house about whom I could never be totally sure: I had met her when she was only a little bigger than the sage plant, they had said to me, "Meet the baby girl," and, smelling her knees—hers, but smaller back then—I had asked myself from that first encounter, "It couldn't be a cat?" Well, in all our years living together, that doubt had never really left me.

The coffee was ready; the announcer was about to bring it to her father, when he came into the kitchen with the toolbox. I hadn't heard him coming either: with the grumbling of the coffeepot, it was hard to pick up the slippered steps. I can't even describe how nimbly she slid the shoe she was still holding under her shirt the moment the old man appeared. I sat myself on the table behind the sugar bowl in order to give the old man his seat; I was also interested in following the conversation from up close: after all, I was in the know about that superfluous bulge between the announcer's breasts.

Rarely did the old man drink his eleven o'clock coffee in the kitchen. Usually they brought it to him in his rooms, whichever one he was in, or in the garden—he'd drink it in two sips, absorbed in the work that needed to be finished. He'd say thank you as he put down the small empty mug, say it with his lips wet with coffee, and go right back to looking after the roses or whatever it was he was doing.

In my current position on the table, I had in front of me the face of the old man and his voice with that coffee taste. The announcer's voice, meanwhile, came at me from behind; every time she spoke, a little bit of shoe spoke too, saying, "You couldn't let someone give you a hand?"

She slurred her words as she said this, without knowing what work her father had been doing in there.

The old man replied soon after: he didn't like to answer, especially in the morning; if he spoke, he spoke as if to himself.

"You could hear the racket all the way up there," the announcer went on.

Up there meant the attic floor: she had lived there since Nabucco had gotten married; but the kitchen was the same for everyone.

The voice in front added something brief; the one behind was ready to go on, but for longer this time. Then the old man spoke again, then his daughter, then I think only the old man spoke; or maybe he coughed without speaking anymore, and I was waking up and regaining my bearings right away: the cough in front, the announcer's silence behind; I was convinced that my being there did them good.

Now and then the announcer counted my vertebrae, rubbing them with her fingertips, probably without realizing it—I let her do it, it was an unthinking habit like coiling and uncoiling a lock of hair. Her hands seemed fairly clammy, maybe she had just gotten out of bed.

I turned around to smell her face, but what I mostly got was the smell of the hidden shoe, so I roamed around the kitchen aimlessly, the tiles had a clean scent; I calmly headed toward the hallway, maybe to go up to the announcer's room. The clock pendulum made the sound it always did in front of the hanging overcoats, in front of the umbrellas: you could get lost just looking inside it—not that I was foolish enough to think I could stop its clockwork, an impossible feat from this side of the glass. But to push a snout up against it, there between the brass pendulum and the winder—in those oscillations of time, minute after minute—I saw the essence of things spring forth; I saw the soul of a cat, not body nor breath but a semblance of dark hair and whiskers barely recognizable, the glistening of an iris, I moved away and it moved away; the soul of an overcoat came out of it, not material, not fabric, but the face of motionlessness, the idea of an umbrella, it was there and it wasn't there, it took less than nothing to make it vanish.

I hurried up the stairs—now I had decided and I no longer looked back. On the second-floor landing I thought I made out someone yawning, I don't remember, I went straight into the attic: jackpot: she was there, against the lamp, but I couldn't reach her, I jumped onto the windowsill so I'd be ready, the windowsill was narrow and cluttered with things, and in my haste I knocked over the ashtray; it fell to the ground but I don't think it broke, and in the meantime the housefly spun three times toward the sink, came back to the lamp, now I was following her from up close, it was a matter of seconds, she looked for a way out, looked for the light of day, flailed against the glass and she was mine; I gave a look around me, I let her go and again she made it to the lamp, more frenziedly this time, and I ignored her, it was a sure shot, I gave a glance at the bed which was still disheveled, I followed her with my eyes, she was on the nightstand and was strolling nonchalantly on the alarm clock; I waited too, I had lain down on the floor, my muscles feeling sluggish, I felt like playing at being the young cat who rolls around on the floor, I took the fly, I wanted to roll around before her eyes, I spat her onto the carpet three centimeters away, she was still alive and I started to lie down and stretch out on my back, I shifted onto my side pushing myself with my paws, I liked keeping those three centimeters of distance, no more and no less; and when I heard the announcer coming up, I popped the fly into my mouth, and it was like a feather in my cap.

Translator's Note

In Anna Felder's 1974 novel *La disdetta* (*Unstill Life with Cat*) a shrewd and sleepy house cat observes the members of his human family after they receive an unexpected eviction notice. The playful and formally inventive novel consists of revelatory moments seen through an intimate and unconventional lens, as the fragile dynamics of the family—an old man living under the same roof as his daughter ("the announcer"), son ("Nabucco"), and daughter-in-law ("the singing teacher")—are thrown off balance in a rapidly changing world. In the translated excerpt, which includes the novel's first and third chapters, I have tried to honor Felder's animated and poetically rhythmic style, with words and things appearing obfuscated and, at the same time, revitalized, while the book's feline narrator drifts in and out of consciousness. Felder's charged and often protean use of language is even reflected in the title of the book, since a "disdetta" means a "notice" (concerning, in this case, the termination of a lease) as well as a "misfortune" or "stroke of bad luck." The English title, which again offers a play on words, takes inspiration from Italo Calvino, who praised the novel as "a way of narrating through objects, almost still lifes; or a visual mapping of space, a 'mise-en-scène' of moments from daily life that's intriguing and accomplished, reminiscent of contemporary poetry." Most of all, I wanted to highlight in translation what Calvino defined as the book's "restrained yet constant humor" and its "very original linguistic flavor."

Bottle to the Sea (Epilogue to a Story)

Julio Cortázar
translated from the Spanish by Harry Morales
LitMag

Dear Glenda, this letter won't be sent through the ordinary chan-
nels because nothing between us can be sent that way, partaking in
the social rite of the envelopes and the post office. It would rather be
as if I were to place it in a bottle and drop it in the waters of the San
Francisco Bay, along which border the house I'm writing you from
is perched; as if I were to fasten it to the neck of one of the seagulls
that pass by like lashes of shadow in front of my window and for a
moment darkens the keyboard of this typewriter. But in any case, a let-
ter addressed to you, to Glenda Jackson in some part of the world that
will probably continue being London; like many letters, like many sto-
ries, there are also messages that are bottles to the sea and enter into
those slow, prodigious sea changes that Shakespeare chiseled in *The
Tempest* and that inconsolable friends would inscribe such a long time
afterwards on the tombstone under which sleeps the heart of Percy
Bysshe Shelley in the cemetery in Caio Cestio, Rome.

That's the way, I think, intimate communications take place, slow
bottles roam in slow seas, just like this letter which searches for you by
your real name will slowly make its way to you, no longer the Glenda
Garson who was also you, but that modesty and affection changed
without changing her, exactly the way you change without changing
from one movie to another. I write to that woman who breathes under
so many masks, including the one I invented so as not to offend her,

and I write to her because now you too have communicated with me under my writer masks. That's why we've earned the right to talk to each other like that, now that without the slightest possibility imaginable your reply just arrived, your own bottle to the sea shattering on the rocks of this bay to fill me with a delight in which something below pulsates like fear, a fear that doesn't silence the delight, that turns it into panic, places it outside of all flesh and all time like you and I have undoubtedly desired each in our own way.

It's not easy to write you this because you don't know anything about Glenda Garson, but at the same time things occur as if I had to uselessly explain something to you that is somehow the reason for her reply; everything occurs as if on different planes, in a duplication that renders absurd any ordinary contact procedure. We're writing or acting for third parties, not for us, and that's why this letter takes the form of a text that will be read by third parties and perhaps never by you, or perhaps by you but only on some distant day, in the same way that your reply has already been seen by third parties while I just received it three days ago via a merely coincidental voyage. I think that if things occur like that, it would be useless to attempt direct contact; I think that the only possibility of telling her this is by directing it once again to those who are going to read it as literature, one story inside another, a coda to something that seemed destined to end with that perfectly definitive closure that to me should contain the good stories. And if I break from the norm, if in my own way I'm writing you this message, perhaps the one that you'll never read is the one that is compelling me, the one that perhaps you're asking me to write to you.

Acknowledge, then, what you couldn't acknowledge and nevertheless acknowledge. It's been exactly two weeks since Guillermo Schavelzon, my editor in México, handed me the first copies of a book of stories that I wrote during these recent times and that bears the title of one of them, *We Love Glenda So Much*. Stories in Spanish, of course, and that will only be translated into other languages in the coming years, stories that this week are just beginning to circulate in México and that you haven't been able to read in London, where otherwise I'm hardly read and much less in Spanish. I have to tell you about one of them feeling sorry at the same time, and in that resides the ambiguous horror that strolls through all of this, the uselessness of doing so because you, in a manner that only the story can insinuate, already knows it. Against all reason, against reason itself, the reply that I just received proves it to me and compels me to do what I'm doing in the face of absurdity, if this is absurd, Glenda, and I think that it is not, although neither you nor I can know what it is.

You'll remember then, even if you can't remember something that you've never read, something whose pages still retain the moistness of the printing ink, which in that story is about a group of friends from Buenos Aires who belong to a secret club fraternity and share the love and admiration that they feel for you, for that actress that is named Glenda Garson in the story, but whose theatrical and cinematic career is denoted with sufficient clarity so that anyone who is deserving can recognize her. The story is very simple: The friends love Glenda so much that they can't tolerate the scandal that some of her movies are below the perfection that all great love postulates and needs, and that the mediocrity of certain directors mars that which you had undoubtedly sought while filming them. Like all narration that proposes a catharsis, which culminates in a purifying sacrifice, this one is allowed to transgress verisimilitude in search of a deeper and more ultimate truth; hence the club does what is necessary to appropriate the copies of the less perfect movies and edits them where a simple deletion or a barely noticeable change in the montage will repair the original unforgivable ineptitude. I suppose that you, like them, don't worry about the despicable practical impossibilities of an operation that the story describes without cumbersome details; loyalty and money simply do their thing, and one day the club can finish the task and enter the happiness of the seventh day. The happiness especially because at that moment you announce your retirement from the theatre and cinema, unknowingly perfecting and bringing to a close a work that reiteration and time would have ended up tarnishing.

Without knowing it . . . Ah, I'm the author of the story, Glenda, but now I can't confirm what seemed so clear to me when I wrote it. Now I've received your reply, and something that has nothing to do with reason compels me to acknowledge that the retirement of Glenda Garson was somewhat strange, almost forced, by the proper end of the unknown and remote club's task. But I continue to tell you the story even though its end seems horrible to me since I have to relate it to you, and it's impossible not to do so since you're in the story, since everyone in México has known the story for ten days and above all because you know it too. Simply, a year later Glenda Garson decides to return to the cinema, and the friends from the club read the news with the overwhelming certainty that it will no longer be possible to repeat a process that they feel has ended, definitive. They have only one way left to defend perfection, the apex of bliss achieved with such difficulty: Glenda Garson will fail to appear in the advertised movie, the club will do what is necessary and forever.

All of this, you see, is a story from a book, with some elements of the fantastic or the unusual that coincide with the tone of the other stories from that volume that my editor handed me on the eve of my departure from México. The reason the book bears that title is simply because to me none of the other stories had that somewhat nostalgic and romantic resonance that your name and your image awaken in my life since one afternoon, in the Aldwych Theatre in London, I saw you whip the naked torso of Marquis de Sade with the silky cords of your hair. Impossible to know, when I selected that title for the book, that in some way I was separating that story from the rest and placing all of its burden on the cover, just like now in your last movie which I just saw three days ago here in San Francisco, someone has selected a title, *Hopscotch*, someone who knows that the word is the translation for *Rayuela* in Spanish. The bottles have reached their destination, Glenda, but the sea in which they drifted isn't the sea of the ships and the albatross.

Everything happened in a second; ironically, I thought that I had come to San Francisco to conduct a course with students from Berkeley and that we were going to have fun with the coincidence of the title of that movie and the novel that would be one of the topics of study. Then, Glenda, I saw the photograph of the lead actor and for the first time it was fear. Having arrived from México with a book that was advertised with your name, and discovering your name in a movie that is advertised with the title of one of my books, was now worthy of a lovely coincidence among the many similar coincidences which I have experienced. But that wasn't all, that was nothing until the bottle shattered into pieces in the darkness of the living room and I acknowledged the reply, I say reply because I can't nor want to believe that it is vengeance.

It isn't vengeance but a summons on the margin of everything that is admissible, an invitation to a trip that can only be completed in territories outside of every territory. The movie, which I can now say is despicable, is based on a spy novel that has nothing to do with you or me, Glenda, and that's precisely why I thought that behind that rather stupid and conveniently vulgar plot something else was being hidden, something unthinkable since you couldn't have anything to tell me and at the same time yes, because now you were Glenda Jackson and if you had accepted to appear in a movie with that title I couldn't stop feeling that you had done so since Glenda Garson, since the beginnings of that story in which I had named you that. And that the movie had nothing to do with that, that it was just a funny spy comedy, compelled me to think about the obvious, about those secret figures or writings that on a page of any previously agreed newspaper or book refer to words that will convey the message for those who know the key. And it was like that, Glenda, it was exactly like that. Do I need to prove it to you when the author of the message is beyond all proof? If I relay it, it is for the third parties who are going to read my story and see your movie, for readers and viewers who will be the naïve bridges of our messages: a story that has just been edited, a movie that has just premiered, and now this letter that almost indescribably contains them and ends them.

I will abbreviate a summary that little interests us anymore. In the movie you love a spy who has started writing a book titled *Hopscotch* aimed at denouncing the dirty tricks of the CIA, the FBI, and the KGB, pleasant offices for which he has worked and that are now striving to kill him. With a loyalty that feeds on tenderness you will help him fake the accident that will leave him for dead in front of his enemies; peace and security await both of you later in some corner of the world. Your friend publishes *Hopscotch*, which although isn't my novel, should necessarily be titled *Rayuela* when some editor of "bestsellers" publishes it in Spanish. An image toward the end of the movie displays copies of the book in a store window, just like the edition of my novel must have been in some U.S. store windows when Pantheon Books published it years ago. In the story that just appeared in México, I killed him symbolically, Glenda Jackson, and in this movie you collaborate in the equally symbolic disposal of the author of *Hopscotch*. As always, you are young and beautiful in the movie, and your friend is old and a writer like me. With my friends from the club, I understood that only through the disappearance of Glenda Garson would the perfection of our love be established forever; you also knew that your love demanded the disappearance to be fulfilled safely. Now, at the end of this which I have written with the vague horror of something equally vague, I know quite well that in your message there is no vengeance, but an incalculably beautiful symmetry, that the character of my story has just met the character of your movie because you wanted it that way, because only that double simulation of death for love could bring us closer. There, in that territory beyond all compass, you and I are looking at each other, Glenda, while I finish this letter here and you somewhere, I think in London, apply makeup to enter a scene or study the role for your next movie.

Berkeley, California, 29 September 1980

Translator's Note

About eighteen months after my dear mentor Gregory Rabassa passed away, I received a FedEx package from his youngest daughter, Clara. Accompanying a beautiful Christmas card was a photocopy of an unmarked 120-page typescript. Its title was *Deshoras*, dated 1982, two years before its author, Julio Cortázar, passed away.

What a unique Christmas gift! Greg and I had many conversations about Julio and he was unquestionably Greg's favorite writer and considered him a loved member of the Rabassa family—*el gigante Tío Julio*. Several days after receiving the *Deshoras* typescript, I examined the table of contents page and recognized six of the eight stories in the collection. Intrigued by the two unfamiliar stories, I embarked upon a brief period of research into the background of all the stories.

I found a paperback edition of an English translation of *Deshoras* in my personal library titled *Unreasonable Hours*, rendered by the acclaimed translator Alberto Manguel. For some reason, the two unfamiliar stories, "Botella al Mar (Epilogo a un Cuento)" and "Diario para un Cuento," were omitted. Naturally, I became enamored with both stories and was proud to render the first story as "Bottle to the Sea (Epilogue to a Story)," which appears in this volume.

The challenging engagement which I have openly invited as a reader of Cortázar's "Botella al Mar (Epilogo a un Cuento)," I also duly accept as a faithful translator. His knowledge of boxing, cats, American jazz, and French surrealism has prepared the shifting terrain for the trap doors cleverly instilled in his Spanish. Love and the willingness to sit attentively on Cortázar's magic carpet and have the ultimate good luck to reverently accept his challenge as a translator have assisted me in navigating the intimate space between the frontiers of the Spanish and English languages.

First We'll Speak Many Words About God

Almog Behar
translated from the Hebrew by Shoshana Olidort
Asymptote

1.

I am tempted to write a poem that will disavow existence
and give it another chance: I'll write that
the Garden of Eden has not yet been created, a snake
yet anticipates the appearance of Eve, Cain
has not yet risen to murder Abel, the tower of Babel
has not yet been built to split the languages of humankind, the
    Torah
has not yet been given to Moses at Sinai, Gilgamesh
has yet to learn the secrets of his body, Melchizedek
yet walks the streets of the city of Salem, the words I use
yet plead to be heard, for the first time.

2.

Between the follies of man and the follies of heaven
I'll choose the follies of man. God
does not forgive, and sways from mercy to judgment.
We will pull the hairs on our heads toward the heavens
until they come apart. With our feet we will weigh heavily
on the ground that shakes and breaks
until it is healed and there is a place for our heads.

3.
Had I not been born
I'd be all forgetfulness,
without any memory
that I could forget
without any joy
I could regret,
without any life
I could lose.

4.
May the miracle come from any place.

5.
We read books
we write books
and the essence is missing from the book.

6.
My sleep is one sixtieth death
or prophecy, my time is one sixtieth redemption
or catastrophe.

7.
A poet yelled at me:
the poems won't give up their wealth
until life itself gives up its poverty.
After him, an economist got up to yell:
the wealthy won't give up their wealth
lest the poor give up their poverty.

8.
Our rabbis said of a king
one doesn't see him when he gets his hair cut,
and not when he is naked, and not
in the bathhouse, and not when he stands
before a doctor, and not when he fasts or prays,
so that the fear of him will be upon us.
And one doesn't ride on his horse, and one doesn't sit
on his chair, and one doesn't use his scepter, and he, too,
doesn't ride on our horses, and doesn't sit
on our chairs, and doesn't use our scepter,
and he doesn't see us when we get our hair cut,
and naked, and bathing, and being healed,
and fasting, and praying, so that the fear of us will be upon him.

9.
I did not sing the praises of the king, I did not describe
his clothes and his gardens and his palaces and his women, and I
    did not rejoice
in the festive marches in which he passed through the city.
I only counted the skulls that he left to roll in the streets,
I counted a thousand, and ten thousand, and when I finished
    counting
the blood had already dried on all of them, and the flesh had
    been consumed.

10.
Jerusalem shatters toward the heavens, and her stones—
half are sharpened and half are broken.
And we are the offspring of those stones, breaking
and being broken, thrown against each other
we return to the walls to beg forgiveness,

to rest inside them. And we draw close
spirit to spirit to shatter, body to body
to sharpen, we plead that our city not draw close
again, to the heavens, that the heavens not descend upon her.
And we whisper upward, we are the stones
of Jerusalem, and there is no Jerusalem but us,
and we whisper downward,
if you return up above,
we will gather on Jerusalem, to leave her
and no stone will remain standing inside her.

11.
First we'll speak many words about god,
that he is one and primordial and immaterial,
that he is the cause of all existence
and the unmoved mover,
that he is merciful and compassionate, patient and full of love
    and truth,
that he hears prayers and pardons sins,
a jealous god who visits the sins of fathers upon sons
takes revenge and bears grudges and remembers iniquities
and it's he who annihilated the generation of the flood
and Sodom and Gomorrah
and he killed the firstborns of Egypt
before he drowned Pharaoh's army in the sea
and instructed the land to open its mouth
and swallow Korah's assembly
and the houses of Korah's assembly
and decreed death for every Amalekite
and exiled Israel from their land
and destroyed his land
and burned his temple,

he, the mighty, the great, the awesome
our father our king
god on high
god our castigator
possessor of heaven and of earth,
he is the first and the last
he precedes all that is
creates the creation
fashions light and creates darkness
makes peace and his hands are war.

12.
First we'll speak many words
about god,
and later we'll listen
to the silence of our words
we will cease to speak
until we do not know
a thing about god
until we do not know
a thing,
until god will say
a thing about us
many words
about us,
that we are many,
dying and living and dying
corporeal and present
we move, are moved, and make move
are merciful and compassionate
begrudging and vengeful
whispering prayers and listening

remembering and forgetting
replenishing human beings and killing.
We, doers of evil and good
peace and war.

13.
We are a little of god
and he is a little of us.
Quiet, and speaking
revealed, and hiding
killing and singing.

14.
And we are still standing on the burnt margins of god
hoping not to be burned
hoping to burn.

15.
What is scarier:
Death or Eternity?

Translator's Note

I first encountered Almog Behar in 2017, when he delivered a guest lecture at Stanford University, where I was pursuing my doctorate. I interviewed him for the *Los Angeles Review of Books* and was struck by his response to a question I posed about the relationship between poetry and politics. Language, he said, is always political, "it is not natural or neutral," and modern Hebrew in particular bears the marks of nationalist and colonialist ideologies, evident in the forcible "removal of Aramaic, rabbinic Hebrew, Yiddish, Judeo-Arabic, and Judeo-Spanish from the language." Literature, he insisted, can help to rectify this, because "it is able to bring back the memory of the different languages," and other memories, too—of what Behar called a period of "Hebrew-Arabic symbiosis" and of God.

In early 2022, Behar posted several poems on Facebook, all from a new collection that had just been released in Hebrew. I began translating one of the posts, which, as it turned out, was a single stanza from a much longer poem. I emailed Behar my translation, and he sent me a digital copy of the collection, *Rub Salt into Love*. "First We'll Speak Many Words About God" is the first poem in the collection, and I was drawn to it in part because of my own ultra-Orthodox upbringing in a world suffused with the word of God, a world in which too few dare to speak back. I love the way the speaker in this poem takes God to task, leveling the playing field: "We are a little of god / and he is a little of us. / Quiet, and speaking / revealed, and hiding / killing and singing."

Bird-women

Vito Apüshana
translated from the Spanish and Wayuu by Maurice Rodriguez
ANMLY

One afternoon, I happened to see two curlews running.
They passed swiftly by my canopy, singing:
    Leu, leu leu, ma. Leu, leu leu, ma.
There was moon over the red resting of the sun ... and
I saw them get lost on the road that goes to the jagüey[1] of
    Mariirop.
Late at night a dream occurred within me ... filled with
    bird-women:
I was Jierü-witush, the azulejo-woman, knitting with all
    the colors of time
Jierü-wawaachi, the dove-woman, was calling her children:
      "Bring life here!"
      "Bring life here!"
Jierü-shotti, the owl-woman, was stalking from the fire
    of her eyes the desired man
Jierü-chünü'ü, the hummingbird-woman, was restoring the flowers
    of the forgotten dreams ...
many birds and many women
Jierü-kaarai, the curlew-woman, over there, swollen with
    omens in every beat of her heart
Jierü-wulu'ui, the turpial-woman, was sharing the cool water

---

1. Traditional water ponds/wells used to store and distribute rainwater primarily used during periods of prolonged drought.

of laughter
Jierü-iisho, the cardinal-woman, was bearing the environment
　　　on her ash-red wings.
When I woke up, I told my mother about the dream . . . and she smiled
　　　without looking at me:
"Ah, she is a wainpirai[2]!"
And since then, I have been discovering the hidden feathers
of the women who shelter us.

---

2. Singing bird, or mockingbird, greatly admired by the Wayuu.

Translator's Note

I discovered "Bird-women" among a collection of Vito's work titled *Antiguos recién llegados* (2019), which guides us through the arid dreamscape of La Guajira, Colombia, where the Wayuu have preserved the spirit of the land and their way of life for centuries.

Whereas Vito's position as a cultural ambassador and human rights activist in the region addresses contemporary Wayuu struggles, his poetic work primarily explores cultural practices, the natural world, and a spiritual/ancestral connection to the land. "Bird-women" is just one example of how his references to natural fauna endemic to La Guajira, sites of spiritual significance, and spiritual beliefs help protect both the Wayuu and their Indigenous language. That's why retaining essential Wayuu terminology is as integral to my translations of Vito's poetry as it is to the author himself, who also retains much of the Wayuu in his self-translations to Spanish. But Vito doesn't merely practice resistance and cultural preservation through his use of bilingualism. It's also present in this choral voice laced throughout all his work.

"Bird-women" may be written in first-person, but there's nothing singular about the "I" speaking to us. Enveloped within a dream cradled by the women who weave together the fabric of Wayuu life, this "I" becomes a collective. Vito is undoubtedly the author of this work, but he's the first to admit that these words aren't his alone. They're also a blend of dreams, experiences, and stories echoed through time and space by family, friends, and ancestors.

I'm grateful to continue this echoing through translation for audiences unfamiliar with his work and Wayuu culture. My hope is that

"Bird-women" acts as a window through which we may respectfully visit La Guajira, and that the publication of Indigenous writing may multiply like the feathers in this poem.

Grazing Land

Leonidas
translated from the Greek by Sherod Santos
Gettysburg Review

Unherded through the icy twilight,
in ones and twos the slow-gaited cattle
descend from the drifted hills. Snow-blind
and blackened by a lightning strike,
the cowherd sits upright by an ilex tree.

Translator's Note

An impoverished wanderer, Leonidas's hundred or so surviving poems made an important contribution to the early development of what's known today as the lyric poem, a form that brought the life-size human figure out from the shadow of heroes and gods. Tuned to the language of the marketplace and harbor, the lovers' bed, the temple grounds, the lyric made everyday human life a subject worthy of poetry.

It's fair to say that in "Grazing Land" nothing out of the ordinary happens—certainly nothing dramatic or life-changing or intellectually demanding. What's more, it presents itself plainly in a quiet voice. Plutarch remarked that "painting is silent poetry, and poetry is painting that speaks," and I think Leonidas's poem is a good example. Its vitality lies in the interplay between the visual image it casts upon the eye, and the significance it expresses through something the language doesn't say that a reader still somehow manages to get.

Of course, translation of classical poetry is a matter of great debate, for its canonical status awakens in us an instinctual reluctance to tamper. Literary translators are renegades in that regard, for the work's aim is to preserve the sensory experience of the poetry itself, to maintain the belief that something beautiful once can go on being beautiful still. To put it more simply: to evoke rather than to mimic has been my general rule.

Two Mapuche-Huilliche Poems

Jaime Huenún Villa
translated from the Spanish by Cynthia Steele
World Literature Today

ÜL **OF CATRILEO**

Matías Catrileo Quezada was killed at point-blank range on January 3, 2008, in the village of Yeupeco, commune of Vilcún, region of La Araucanía. The twenty-two-year-old activist was participating in a peaceful takeover of land when he was shot by policeman Walter Ramírez, who was carrying a nine-millimeter Uzi submachine gun.

We won't turn over the body, no:
this is the death they have left us,
the bullets that sliced through the dawn
on Matías Catrileo's river
in Vilcún.

But Llaima Volcano is burning for you
and the ashes of your hidden eyes
are writing in the snow
the rage and the mystery
of a people with no more forests or arms,
surrounded by tanks and tear-gas bombs,
seated at the bench of the Royal Indian Court
of modernity.

Let night's ferrymen come
flying over the water
and the blue maidens
who heal the warrior's wounds
with their voices.

We won't turn over the body
to the judge's forensics,
nor to the cameras that can never have
their fill of the dead.

We won't turn over the body, say
the ambushed pumas of Vilcún,
we are the tomb of Matías Catrileo,
the grass of his bloodied hands,

his parents' river of justice
the deep roots of his light
in the yellow lands of Yeupeco.

JAIME MENDOZA COLLÍO LOSES HIS WAY
AND SINGS IN THE INVISIBLE FORESTS OF
REQUÉM PILLÁN

Jaime Mendoza Collío was killed by the Chilean police on August 12, 2009, when he was twenty-four years old. Requém Pillán, the community he came from, is located eighty-four kilometers to the northeast of the city of Temuco.

Where does the thread of a long look come from?
And the color of death in the ocean flowers?

Yes, I was born dark like a scarab
and dark I will die, under the light of the sun.

The terrestrial machines barely nod to me
as I search through my father's feverish mud.

Bones ringing out, moons circulating
over children fleeing from blue horseflies.

Soon I will order the islands into existence,
soon I will set out for the Land Up Above.

And I'll tell the wild river to dream within my bloodstream,
and I'll tell the red larch trees to light up the air.

Now I'm climbing a path leading to the summit,
to hidden forests where I revive and sing.

Death on the cusp of dawn burns in the mountains,
the light shatters the window like a wound.

Translator's Note

I first encountered Jaime Huenún through his book *Reducciones*, which I found online and which provides a sweeping overview of the centuries of violent conquest and appropriations of Indigenous persons and lands by Spanish and Chilean colonizers. I approached Huenún through a mutual friend, Chilean poet Sergio Mansilla. Since I do not speak the Huilliche language, my collaborations with Huenún, which now include four books of poetry, have involved extensive back and forth correspondence between us, as well as intensive readings regarding Huilliche language and philosophy. Huenún has been an ideal, generous interlocutor, patient with all my inquiries and extremely detailed and precise in his explanations. Recently the process has been complicated by Huenún's health crises and extended stays in hospitals. Throughout this time, he has continued to respond promptly with whatever information is required by a variety of journals and presses.

[Untitled]

Saeb Tabrizi
translated from the Persian by Kayvan Tahmasebian
    and Rebecca Ruth Gould
The Margins

I hear God's promise of forgiveness in the babbling wine.
From the rubab, I hear the clang of Paradise's gate.

This is the difference when we hear:
you hear the door closing, I hear it opening.

Why not lie, like a rug, at the threshold of the tavern?
I hear hearts throb there beneath the dust.

The rose-colored wine running through my winding veins
sounds to me more lucid than the stream's burbling.

I see lucidly the veiled phantoms.
I hear the gazelle's footfalls in my dreams.

Everything I see unveiled sings
a song that dyes the gallows' rope.

I hear Gabriel, archangel of love, fluttering
every moment in the cracks of my restless heart.

Moonlight smells like jasmine.
Has it kissed my beloved's cheeks?

Your garments smell like smoke.
Have you been at the feast of the heated hearts?

Such raw words, Saeb, come from such dark hearts:
the ones who feel protected by that sun.

Translators' Note

We—an American and an Iranian—met in Isfahan on a late August day in 2016. We walked from Charbagh Boulevard to Saeb's tomb, along Niasarm brook (*mādī*, as it is called by the locals). During the very first hours of our meeting, we discussed poetry and its translation. Afterward, across continents and time zones, our cotranslation flourished through hours of discussions and drafts exchanged through emails and messages.

Saeb's ghazal poses significant challenges to an English translation. A delicate irony opens the ghazal, which personifies the bubbling wine as though repeating the Arabic phrase "*huwa al-ghafur*," meaning "God will forgive." The words refer to the prohibition on drinking wine in Islam. The second line challenges a similar interdiction imposed by Islamic jurists on playing and listening to music. The line indirectly likens the sound of the *rabab*, a lute-like musical instrument played in Central and South Asia, to the squeaky sound of Paradise's gate. The heretical irony that is implied by the first verse is taken up immediately by the second verse, which is crystalized like a beautiful and succinct proverb on the dialectic of hope and despair, optimism and pessimism. The verse also epitomizes the antinomy between the poet and the jurist: one interprets the squeak as sign of Paradise's door opening, the other hears it as the sound of its closing.

A literal translation would not have served Saeb's poem well. The poet praises wine for its power in making a seer of the poet: one who paradoxically sees the unseeable (literally "the transparence of the veiled brides of imagination," a recurring metaphor in Persian Sufism) and who hears the unhearable (literally "the footsteps of the deer in dreams"). We hope our translation conveys a trace of Saeb's ghazal in its perpetual receding.

The mistress of the house

ko ko thett
translated from the Burmese by the author
Tupelo Quarterly

Lest she upset the cosmic balance
she gave a second thought to the cobweb
at the corner of the kitchen ceiling.

On the radio she heard
four prisoners had been hanged
in a remote dictator land.

A woman does house chores.
A tyrant kills dissent.

She decided
to leave the cobweb to
the stay-at-home
layabout of a husband.

Translator's Note

My piece is a rather straightforward self-translation. The title, "The mistress of the house," is a loan translation of "အိမ်ရှင်မ [eain-shin-ma]," a three-syllable word wherein each of the syllables has a meaning (eain for house, shin for owner, and ma for lady). The word also means "wife" and reflects the fact that Burmese women usually man their homes. The Burmese Buddhist notion, lokapala, a Pali word, I decided to render into English as "cosmic balance." The poem was inspired by the executions of three political dissidents in a Myanmar jail in 2022.

The Reeling City

Najwa Bin Shatwan
translated from the Arabic by Mona Zaki
Michigan Quarterly Review

I knocked on the door and entered the office of Colonel Hamid, the official in charge of criminal investigations in Benghazi. He was a rotund man with a thick beard, stern features, and sunglasses that contributed to his intimidating demeanor as evening descended on the city, thus making the sunglasses appear unnecessary. He looked up and stared, surprised, and asked, as one would expect from a man in security, "Who are you? What brings you here? Can't you see all the files and cases in front of me?"

"Yes, I do, I'm seeing everything since the attack on my life. I'm the corpse of a Libyan citizen dumped on Zeit Street."

The Colonel took a good look at me. "Ohh . . . Zeit Street is full of corpses! Are you by any chance Mr. Faraj al-Jahawi?"

"No."

"If not, then his son, Tewfiq al-Jahawi?"

"No. But why these two names in particular?"

"Because ustaaz Faraj is the only one who speaks in formal Arabic, being one of the founders of the Friends of the Arabic Language Society in Benghazi. I thought you could be him or his son Tewfiq, unless you caught the virus of speaking in formal language."

"I don't know, really. It's your job to find out who I am. I lost my name after my assassination, and I would like to retrieve it. It's shameful to me as a dead person to be deprived of my identity and to be treated as an anonymous corpse. I am Libyan."

The Colonel answered touchily, "Your file has not yet arrived."

"I want to know the identity of those who assassinated me. A black jeep pursued me in the dark, four men got out, kidnapped me, and took me to an unspecified location where they tortured me before killing and then desecrating my corpse."

"Didn't you recognize any of them?"

"Unfortunately, Mr. Colonel, I did not, nor did I have with me a pair of sunglasses like those that help you weigh the facts and reach the truth."

"You mean to say that you sat with them, they tortured and humiliated you—and all the while you didn't manage to know who they were? That's funny!"

"Yes, it's hilarious, otherwise how would all this happen to me?"

The Colonel started to stroke his thick beard as a sign of his having a think. "But according to the investigations that I have here, you've been dead since 1988—that is before the Revolution by some time. In other words, Qaddafi killed you, so what brought you to Zeit Street?"

"That's why it's funny. It's true that Zeit Street has been opened by the new Revolution, not the old one, and to be specific, during the military control of your splendid era, but death is older than the new revolution in this country, and it gets revitalized every once in a while. And here it has happened to me a second time and I want to follow up on the matter of my soul—this is of interest to me."

The Colonel sighed deeply, slowly exhaling the word "Souuuuuul." Then he sat up. "Come back next week. We could have some results by then regarding investigations of the killers."

"And why next week?"

"Can't you see how busy I am with the security of the city around the Christmas festivities?"

"Do these festivities, God forbid, threaten the people of the city in the same way that Zeit Street and the Safsafah project do?"

"Yes, as a matter of fact. Christian celebrations do threaten the morality of Benghazi inhabitants, and our customs and traditions. My responsibility is to maintain security."

Before I left I said, "May God protect Libya and its people."

•

On my way out, I saw in the waiting room several handcuffed corpses with marks of having been tortured. They had been hanged and abandoned on Zeit Street. It was clear that they'd been visiting the security headquarters regularly to learn of the latest news regarding their deaths. One of the corpses was Nabila, who recognized me.

"Hello ustaaz! I didn't expect to see you here! What a coincidence! How are you doing?"

"Thanks be to God. Much better after my assassination. I got rid of money, debt installments, and a life of standing in queues, not to mention the daily crises of life."

"Are you part of the Safsafah project or the Abyar?"

"Much, much older, why do you ask?"

"You should thank God you're not from the Abyar group! Man, the treatment there is worse than in any part of the world."

At that point the corpse of a young man whose chest was riddled with bullets like a couscous sieve interjected, "I've been coming here for years, and so many colonels have come and gone, as have the truth committees. They almost give birth to one another to no avail."

Our soft conversation tempted another corpse to come out of its silence: "Maybe it's the lack of resources."

"That doesn't stop them from buying cars, expensive four-wheel drives, as if these would uncover the truth about our deaths and solve the lack of security in this bereaved city."

"The Colonel himself has a whole fleet of luxury cars that you only see in Mafia or action movies."

Another corpse leaning on its head added, "And despite that, not one step forward has been taken in any investigation. They never mounted security cameras, nor the electronic gates around Benghazi . . . really strange!"

The personal security detail of the Colonel arrived and asked us to leave quickly. We asked one another what could have happened. Each one claimed to know the real cause behind the emergency, providing us with nine different versions that either contradicted or affirmed one another. No one had the right to refute any of them.

The Colonel left his office in a hurry, his official boots echoing, sounding much like the sound my Turkish mother made as she ground nutmeg with her pestle. This was clearly a security matter. The corpses rushed to the window overlooking the entrance of the building to find out more. The Colonel got into his impressive military vehicle, which moved amid a loud phalanx of cars.

•

Some corpses suspected that someone could have broken the norm and, God forbid, died a natural death, or that a new street for corpses had emerged without the necessary military permits. From our experience in the streets of death, we guessed this could be the reason. There was a rumor, though, that a corpse flying across the skies of Benghazi managed to recognize its killer without the help of the Department of Internal Security or the services of Colonel Hamid. It was considered necessary to halt its progress before the phenomenon spread and more corpses found their killers.

One corpse asked its neighbor, "What do you think if we took to flying?" The other answered, "I fear bullets."

"If you were put in prison, you would not be killed with explosives or mines, but you would die by other means and wouldn't need to recognize your killer. When the State puts you in a body bag, it places its own seal that maintains you died by torture, isn't that so?"

"Yes."

"Then you don't need to fly."

A soldier came and called out, "Come on now, go back to the graveyard, everyone! The Security Apparatus is working from outside its offices today." An anxious corpse eager to know its fate asked, "When will Colonel Hamid return?"

"The Colonel will not be returning today. He is attending the burning of a large quantity of hashish in the port. He's supervising the operation himself."

The corpses hugged one another happily. "We'll sniff the hashish for free," they laughed. "Fiesta, fiesta! Let's go!"

Only one ancient, dignified corpse remained silent and then said dryly, "How often have I gotten used to this free hashish thanks to the State! I'm taking off to the port right now."

The skies were filled with people, so many more than those on earth below. But the old ones—from among all God's creatures— were the fastest.

Translator's Note

I heard an interview of Najwa Bin Shatwan where she talked about the background and the research for her novel *Yards of Slaves* and the difficulty of finding material related to slaves and slavery in Libya. I was captivated by the subject matter and the need of the author to uncover a part of Libyan history that was painful and not easy to find. I then read her collection of short stories *Sudfa Jariyah* ("An Ongoing Coincidence") published in Beirut in 2019.

CONTRIBUTORS' BIOGRAPHIES

Kareem James Abu-Zeid, Ph.D., is an Egyptian-American free-lance translator of poets and novelists from across the Arab world who translates from Arabic, French, and German. He has received the 2022 Sarah Maguire Prize for Poetry in Translation, a 2018 NEA translation grant, PEN Center USA's 2017 translation prize, *Poetry* magazine's 2014 translation prize, a Fulbright research fellowship, and residencies from the Lannan Foundation and the Banff Center, among other honors. He is also the author of the book *The Poetics of Adonis and Yves Bonnefoy: Poetry as Spiritual Practice*. The online hub for his work is www.kareemjamesabuzeid.com.

Edith Adams (Phoenix, 1992) is a literary translator working pri-marily between Spanish and English. She is a Ph.D. Candidate in Comparative Literature at the University of Southern California and is an alumna of the Bread Loaf Translators' Conference and the Banff International Literary Translation Centre. Her translation work has appeared in *Guernica*, *Latin American Literature Today*, *New England Review*, *Northwest Review*, *Words Without Borders*, and elsewhere.

Samson Allal is a Moroccan-American poet. His work plays with some of the histories, stories, the rhythms of mythology, the choirs of meaning, that move, migrate, between North Africa, Europe, and the Middle East, and settle like a flock on the little boulder of his unknow-ing head. His poetics spring from a music of relation: a New World remix. Samson Allal's poetry has appeared in *Black Renaissance Noire*,

Rip Rap Journal, Oxford Magazine, Gulf Coast, Girl Blood Info, and *Poetry.*

Muntather Alsawad was educated in his home country of Iraq, where he studied literary criticism and published critical papers, stories, and poems in Arabic. Since arriving in the U.S., he has devoted himself to translating Iraqi poetry into English, as well as writing English-language poetry of his own. He lives in Portland, Maine. His translations have appeared in *Asymptote, Samovar, MAYDAY, Last Stanza, AzonaL,* and others.

Jesús Amalio Lugo is a writer and a biomedical engineer. He has received honorable mentions for the Roberto Bolaño poetry prize (2017), the JL Gabriela Mistral poetry prize (2018), and the Rafael Cadenas poetry prize (2018), and he received second place for the Fernando Santiván story contest (2019). From Coro, Venezuela, he now resides in the south of Chile.

Stine Su Yon An is a poet, literary translator, and performer based in New York City. She holds an M.F.A. in Literary Arts from Brown University and a B.A. in Literature from Harvard College. Her translations have appeared in *World Literature Today, Black Sun Lit, Waxwing, The Southern Review, Chicago Review,* and elsewhere. She is the recipient of fellowships and grants from the American Literary Translators Association, the Corporation of Yaddo, and the PEN/ Heim Translation Fund.

Izidora Angel is a Bulgarian-born writer and literary translator in Chicago. She is the author of two book-length translations and an NEA grant recipient for her work on Yordanka Beleva's *Keder.* Izidora's writing has appeared in *Astra, Electric Literature, Two Lines, Chicago Reader,* and elsewhere. Her work has been recognized by English

PEN, Art Omi, Bread Loaf, the Rona Jaffe Foundation, and others. She's a 2023 Elizabeth Kostova Foundation Fellow for her in-progress memoir of growing up in the last days of communism, the meteoric rise and agonizing ruin of a mercurial father, and a family's forced, prolonged separation.

The original author of a Hymn to Ra is an **anonymous scribe** who lived in the second millennium before the birth of Jesus Christ in the land now known as Egypt. This scribe, like most tradespeople today, was not encouraged to chisel their name into the tablet they inscribed. Ancient Egyptian authors were stone masons, sculptors, who worked with the Pharaohs, the high priests, or any person who had the resources to commission a work of hieroglyphs. In the case of a Hymn to Ra it is likely that the Pharaoh Intef II dictated the poem to the scribe.

Vito Apüshana is a writer, human rights activist, and former professor at the University of La Guajira from the town of Carraipía, La Guajira, Colombia. His most recent collection of poetic work, *Antiguos recién llegados,* was published by Sílaba in 2019. His earlier works are *Contrabandeo sueños con alijunas cercanos* (1992) and *En las hondonadas maternas de la piel* (2010); others can be found online and in magazines like *Número* (Bogotá), *Casa de las Américas* (Havana), *Le Poésie* (Paris), *Americas Quarterly* (New York), and *La Jornada* (Mexico City).

Madeleine Arenivar is a translator and editor. She specializes in academic and, more recently, literary prose from Spanish. Her literary translations have been published in *Another Chicago Magazine, Latin American Literature Today,* and *Los Angeles Review,* and have been shortlisted for the PEN Presents program. Madeleine has degrees from Vassar College and the Latin American Faculty of Social Sciences

(FLACSO) Ecuador. She received a Katharine Bakeless Nason scholarship for emerging writers to attend Bread Loaf Translators' Conference in 2022. She lives in Quito, Ecuador.

Rolla Barraq was born in Mosul, Iraq, in 1985, a city that was invaded and occupied by ISIS from 2014–2017. In 2018, her poetry collection, *What Has Arrived from It,* won the competition of the General Union of Writers in Iraq. She has a Ph.D. in Arabic literature and lives in Mosul, where she is leader of the Poetry Club.

Almog Behar is a poet, novelist, translator, and researcher based in Jerusalem. Behar has published six books, the latest being על האהבה *כדי שהמלת יתפזר* (*Rub Salt into Love*; Hakibbutz Hameuchad, 2021). His other books are: צמאון בארות (*Well's Thirst*; Am Oved, 2008); יהוד אנא מן אל- *מושך מן הלשון* (*I am one of the Jews*; Babel, 2009); הסוהר- *חוט* (*A Thread Drawing from the Tongue*; Am Oved, 2009); and *שירים לאסירי בתי* (*Poems for the Prisoners*; IndieBook, 2016). His novel רחלה וחזקל׳ (*Rachel and Ezekiel*; Keter, 2010) was translated into Arabic and published in Cairo in 2016.

Yordanka Beleva is a Bulgarian poet and writer. She is the author of the poetry collections *Peignoirs and Boats* (2002), *Her* (2012), and *Missed Moment* (2017), as well as of the short story collections *The Sea Level of Love* (2011), *Keys* (2015), *Keder* (2018), and *Porcupines Come Out at Night* (2022). Her stories and poems have been translated into English, French, Spanish, German, Turkish, Arabic, and Croatian, and anthologized in multiple collections. Yordanka has been a finalist for and a recipient of multiple national awards for both poetry and prose. Several of her stories have been made into award-winning films.

Najwa Bin Shatwan is a Libyan academic and author. She has written three novels as well as short stories and plays. Her novel *Zareeb* *al-Abeed* (Yards of Slaves) was shortlisted for the 2017 International Prize for Arabic Fiction (IPAF). She obtained her Ph.D. in History from La Sapienza in Rome in 2017.

Natascha Bruce translates fiction from Chinese. Her recent work includes *Lake Like a Mirror* by Ho Sok Fong, *Mystery Train* by Can Xue, and *Owlish* by Dorothy Tse, the latter of which was awarded a 2021 PEN/Heim grant. After several years in Hong Kong, she now lives in Amsterdam.

David M. Brunson is the editor and translator of *A Scar Where Goodbyes Are Written: An Anthology of Venezuelan Poets in Chile* (LSU Press, 2023). His poems and translations have appeared in *Copper Nickel, Mānoa: A Pacific Journal of International Writing, ANMLY, DIAGRAM, Washington Square Review, The Journal of Italian Translation*, and elsewhere. He is the cofounder of *Copihue Poetry*, an online magazine dedicated to publishing poetry in English, Spanish, and in translation.

Hisham Bustani is an award-winning Jordanian author whose work explores the boundaries of fiction and poetry and revolves around the dystopian experience of postcolonial modernity in the Arab world. His writing has been translated into many languages and published in journals and anthologies including *Kenyon Review, The Georgia Review, The Poetry Review, Modern Poetry in Translation, World Literature Today*, and *Best Asian Short Stories*. His collection *The Perception of Meaning* (Syracuse University Press, 2015) received the University of Arkansas Arabic Translation Award, and his most recent book in English translation is *The Monotonous Chaos of Existence* (Mason Jar, 2022).

James Byrne is a poet, editor and translator. His most recent poetry collections from Arc Publications are *Places You Leave* (2021) and

The Caprices (2019). He cotranslated and coedited *I am a Rohingya: Poems from the Camps and Beyond* (Arc, 2020) and *Bones Will Crow: 15 Contemporary Burmese Poets* (Arc, 2012). Byrne is a Reader in Contemporary Literature at Edge Hill University, codirector of EHU Press and International Editor for Arc Publications. He has given readings across the world, including in Libya, and is renowned for his commitment to international poetries.

Charles Cantalupo's work has received support from the Ford and Rockefeller Foundations and the World Bank, and he is coauthor of the historic "Asmara Declaration on African Languages and Literature." His books include translations of Eritrean poetry and literary criticism ranging from Thomas Hobbes to Ngũgĩ wa Thiong'o. He is also the author of a memoir, *Joining Africa*, a collection of essays, *Non-Native Speaker*, and five books of his own poetry—most recently, *Sykes in Africa*, on the photography of Lawrence F. Sykes.

Bernard Capinpin is a poet and translator. He received a PEN/Heim Translation Fund Grant for Edel Garcellano's *A Brief Investigation to a Long Melancholia*. He lives in the Philippines.

Juan Cárdenas is a Colombian art critic, curator, translator, and author of seven works of fiction, most recently the novels *Elástico de sombra* and *Peregrino transparente*. He has translated the works of such writers as William Faulkner, Thomas Wolfe, Gordon Lish, David Ohle, J. M. Machado de Assis, and Eça de Queirós. In 2014, his novel *Los estratos* received the Otras Voces Otros Ámbitos Prize. In 2017, he was named one of the thirty-nine best Latin American writers under the age of thirty-nine by the Hay Festival in Bogotá.

Disney Cardoso is a cosigner of the peace agreement and ex-combatant of the former FARC-EP. She is an early childhood education aid and student of Territorial Public Administration. In addition to the nonfiction account she published in *Naturaleza común: relatos de no ficción de excombatientes para la reconciliación* (2021), her story of experiencing homelessness appears in the volume *Sin habitación propia* (2022).

Daniela Catrileo (Santiago, 1987) is a writer, artist, activist, and professor of philosophy. She is a member of the Colectivo Mapuche Rangiñtulewfü and part of the editorial team for *Yene*, a digital magazine featuring art, writing, and critical thought from across Wallmapu and the Mapuche diaspora. She has published two collections of poetry: *Río herido* (2016) and *Guerra florida* (2018), two chapbooks: *El territorio del viaje* (2017, 2022) and *Las aguas dejaron de unirse a otras aguas* (2020), and a book of short stories: *Piñen* (2019). She also explores other artistic formats such as performance, video art, and sound-visual poetry.

Geet Chaturvedi is a poet, novelist, and essayist. He is one of the most widely read contemporary Hindi writers. He has authored two collections of novellas, three collections of poetry, two books of nonfiction, and a novel. The recipient of numerous literary prizes, including the Syed Haidar Raza fellowship for fiction writing, he was named among the Ten Best Young Writers of India by the *Indian Express*. He won the 2021 Vatayan-UK Literary Award for his contribution to Hindi literature. His works have been translated into twenty-two languages. His Instagram is @geetchaturvedi.

Jeffrey Clapp was raised and educated in New Hampshire and taught for many years at SUNY Dutchess in New York State. He has published poems, stories, and translations in *North American Review, Arkansas Review, Dalhousie Review, Sycamore Review*, et al; several have been reprinted in anthologies. He is a past recipient of the Daniel Morin Poetry Prize from the University of New Hampshire and the Indiana Fiction Prize from Purdue. He lives in South Portland, Maine.

Julio Cortázar was born in Brussels to Argentine parents on August 26, 1914, and raised near Buenos Aires. From 1945 to 1951 he worked as a literary translator for Argentine publishers. In 1951 he moved to France, where he lived permanently. He was also a poet, amateur jazz musician, and the author of more than eighty books in various genres. His novel, *Rayuela* (translated by Gregory Rabassa as *Hopscotch*), was widely praised and earned Cortázar an enthusiastic international following. Considered one of the great modern Latin American authors, he died in Paris on February 12, 1984.

Najwan Darwish (b. 1978) is one of the foremost contemporary Arab poets. His poetry has been hailed around the world as a singular expression of the Palestinian struggle. He has published eight books in Arabic and has been translated into more than thirty languages. Darwish's *Nothing More to Lose* (NYRB, 2014), translated by Kareem James Abu-Zeid, was picked as one of the best books of the year by NPR. His second major collection in English translation, *Exhausted on the Cross* (NYRB Poets, Foreword by Raúl Zurita), received the 2022 Sarah Maguire Prize. Darwish lives between Haifa and his birthplace, Jerusalem.

Lizzie Davis is a writer, editor, and translator from Spanish and Italian to English. Among her translations are Juan Cárdenas's *Ornamental* (a finalist for the 2021 PEN Translation Prize) and *The Devil of the Provinces*; Elena Medel's *The Wonders*, cotranslated with Thomas Bunstead; and works by Pilar Fraile Amador, Aura García-Junco, and Valeria Luiselli. Her cotranslations of Daniela Tarazona's *Divided Island* and *The Animal on the Rock* with Kevin Gerry Dunn are forthcoming from Deep Vellum.

Armen Davoudian is the author of the poetry collection *The Palace of Forty Pillars* (Tin House Books, 2024). His poems and translations from Persian appear in *Poetry* magazine, *The Hopkins Review*, *Yale Review*, and elsewhere. Armen grew up in Isfahan, Iran, and is currently a Ph.D. candidate in English at Stanford University.

A prolific and multifaceted writer, Luis Alberto de Cuenca possesses one of Spain's most distinctive poetic voices. Trained in classical philology, Cuenca has published widely about Latin and Greek authors, but is best known for a large body of accessible, elegant and witty poems. In 2015 he received the National Poetry Prize for *Cuaderno de vacaciones* (Vacation Notebook) and in 2021 he won the prestigious Federico García Lorca International Poetry Prize. He has published more than a dozen poetry collections, most recently *Después del paraíso* (After Paradise). He has gathered his poems in the omnibus volume *Los mundos y los días*, whose most recent edition dates from 2019.

Neil P. Doherty is a translator born in Dublin, Ireland, in 1972 who has resided in Istanbul since 1995. He currently teaches at Bilgi University. He is a translator of Turkish poetry and prose. In 2017 he edited *Turkish Poetry Today*, published in the UK by Red Hand Books. His translations have appeared in *Poetry Wales*, *The Dreaming Machine*, *The Honest Ulsterman*, *Turkish Poetry Today*, *Arter* (İstanbul), *Advaitam Speaks*, *The Seattle Star*, *The Antonym*, *The Enchanting Verses* and *The Berlin Quarterly*. He has recently finished translating a prose work by Enis Batur, one of Turkey's leading writers.

Ashur Etwebi was born in 1952 in Libya. He is one of Libya's leading poets and is also an editor, translator, and painter. Ashur has published nine volumes of poetry and seven volumes of translations. *Above the Hill: Selected Poems* was translated by Brenda Hillman and

Dialla Haidar and published in the U.S. in 2011. Since December 2014 he has lived in Norway after he was attacked by extremists and his house in Tripoli was burned down. He organized (with Khaled Mattawa), the first ever Tripoli International Poetry Festival in 2012.

Eirill Alvilde Falck is a Norwegian-born writer and translator. Her work has been recognized with an Iowa Arts Fellowship and a Zell Fellowship, and with the John Wagner Prize and the Hopwood Award. She is the cofounder of *MQR: Mixtape*, an imprint of *Michigan Quarterly Review*. She collects screams. You can add your scream to her collection by leaving a voicemail message at (424) 226-6734.

Anna Felder (1937, Lugano–2023, Aarau) was one of Switzerland's most acclaimed Italian-language writers. In 2018, she received Switzerland's highest literary honor, the Swiss Grand Award for Literature. Her novel *La disdetta* (*Unstill Life with Cat*) was published by the publishing house Einaudi in 1974, after being selected by editor Italo Calvino, and won the 1975 Schiller Prize.

Zuzanna Ginczanka was born in 1917 into a Russian-speaking Jewish family in Kyiv. Fleeing the Russian Revolution, the family settled in Rivne (then Równe), but she remained stateless throughout her life. Choosing Polish as her language of poetic expression, she published but one collection of verse, *O Centaurach* (On Centaurs, 1936). The present poem was found among manuscripts rescued by Eryk Lipinski from her Warsaw apartment in 1939. Ginczanka was executed by the Nazis in May of 1944. In recent years, interest in Ginczanka's poetry and life has inspired exhibits, collections of her verse, and musical and theatrical performances.

Anita Gopalan is the recipient of a PEN/Heim Translation Fund grant and a fellowship in English literature from the Indian Ministry of

Culture. A graduate in Mathematics and Computer Science, she works as a stock trader and literary translator. Her translations from Hindi include Geet Chaturdevi's *The Memory of Now* (Anomalous Press, 2019) and *Simsim* (Penguin Random House, 2023). She has been published in *AGNI, PEN America, Tupelo Quarterly, World Literature Today, Two Lines, Poetry International Rotterdam, Chicago Review, Words Without Borders, Asymptote, Modern Poetry in Translation, The Common*, and elsewhere. Her Instagram is @anitagopalan16.

Rebecca Ruth Gould is a writer, critic, scholar, and translator. With Kayvan Tahmasebian, she has translated Hasan Alizadeh's *House Arrest* (2022), which was the recipient of a PEN Translates award, *High Tide of the Eyes: Poems by Bijan Elahi* (2019), and Tahmasebian's own poems, *Lecture on Fear and Other Poems* (2019). Her solo translations include Hasan Dehlevi's *After Tomorrow the Days Disappear* (Northwest University Press, 2016). She is also the editor, with Kayvan Tahmasebian, of *The Routledge Handbook of Translation and Activism* (2020). She has published widely on Persian literature, including *The Persian Prison Poem: Sovereignty and the Political Imagination* (2021).

Alice Guthrie is an independent translator, editor, researcher, and curator, specializing in contemporary Arabic literature and media. Her work often focuses on subaltern voices, orality, and queerness/queering. Among various accolades over the years, she has won the Jules Chametzky Translation Prize 2019 for her translation of Gazan author Atef Abu Saif's "The Lottery." Her bilingual editorial and research work aims to be part of the growing movement to decolonize the Arabic-English literary translation sector. She has taught undergraduate and postgraduate Arabic-English translation around and about, including at the University of Birmingham and the University of Exeter, both in the UK.

Jiyar Homer is a translator and editor from Kurdistan, a member of Kashkul, the Center for Arts and Culture at the American University of Iraq, Sulaimani (AUIS), and serves as an editor for the literary magazine *Îlyan*. He speaks Kurdish, English, Spanish, Portuguese, Arabic, and Persian. His translations have appeared in thirty countries, including in *World Literature Today*, *Literary Hub*, *The Brooklyn Rail*, *Periódico de Poesía*, *Círculo de Poesía*, *Buenos Aires Poetry* and *Revista POESIA*. His book-length translations include works by Juan Carlos Onetti, Carlos Ruiz Zafón, Farhad Pirbal, and Sherzad Hassan. He is also a member of Kurdish PEN.

Jaime Huenún Villa is an award-winning Mapuche-Huilliche poet whose books include *Ceremonias* (1999), *Puerto Trakl* (2001), *Reducciones* (2012), *Fanon City Meu* (2014), and *La calle Mandelstam y otros territorios apócrifos* (2016). His latest collection of poetry, *Crónicas de la Nueva Esperanza / Chronicles of New Hope*, is forthcoming in a bilingual version from Lom Ediciones in Santiago.

Catalina Infante Beovic is a Chilean writer, publisher, and bookstore owner. She has written three books of short stories of the Indigenous peoples of Chile, authored the picture book *Dichos redichos* and the artist's book *Postal nocturna*, and published the story collection *Todas somos una misma sombra*. Her debut novel, *La grieta*, was published in 2023 by Emecé, an imprint of Planeta. Her work appears in translation in *World Literature Today*, *Columbia Journal*, and HarperCollins' *Daughters of Latin America: An International Anthology of Writing by Latine Women*. Find more of her work at www.catalinainfantebeovic.com.

Samwai Lam earned her B.A. and M.A. and degrees in comparative literature from the University of Hong Kong. Her art writing has been shortlisted for the International Awards for Art Criticism. Her novels include *White Dirt* (白漬, 2017) and *Moon Phase* (月相, 2020).

A recipient of the Literature Award from the House of Hong Kong Literature, Lam's short stories have appeared in *Fleurs des Lettres* (字花), *SAMPLE*, and *Esquire*. In 2022, she was elected Hong Kong Spotlight Author of the Aesop Queer Library and awarded the Art Critiques Writing Scheme Grant, writing on HK contemporary art through a queer lens.

Jeanine Legato is a translator, interpreter, and researcher based in Bogotá. She specializes in Colombian literary and academic translation, particularly pertaining to issues of human rights and the armed conflict.

Unrecognized in his time, **Leonidas** lived an impoverished life on the coast of Apulia in the third century BCE. Only a hundred or so of his poems still survive, but through them we see that he was little interested in metaphysical issues and took as his subjects the humbler lives of peasants, hunters, carpenters, and weavers, "the community of workers." More at home in a wattle hut than a rich man's house, he declared that "an old man is content with two barley cakes and some sea salt."

Alana Marie Levinson-LaBrosse is a poet, translator, and the Founding Director of Kashkul, the center for arts and culture at the American University of Iraq, Sulaimani (AUIS). She was a 2022 NEA Fellow, the first ever working from the Kurdish. Her writing has appeared in *Poetry, Modern Poetry in Translation, World Literature Today, Plume, Epiphany,* and *The Iowa Review*. Book-length works include Kajal Ahmad's *Handful of Salt* (2016), Abdulla Pashew's *Dictionary of Midnight* (2019), and Farhad Pirbal's *The Potato Eaters* (2024).

Dmitri Manin is a physicist, programmer, and poetry translator. His translations from English and French into Russian have appeared in several book collections. Among his latest work are a complete translation of Ted Hughes's *Crow* (Jaromír Hladík Press, 2020) and Allen Ginsberg's *Howl, Kaddish and Other Poems* (Podpisnie Izdaniya, 2021). Dmitri's Russian-to-English translations have been published in journals (*Cardinal Points, Delos, The Café Review, Metamorphoses,* et al), in Maria Stepanova's *The Voice Over* (CUP, 2021) and in the anthology *Disbelief: 100 Russian Anti-War Poems* (Smokestack Books, 2023). In 2017, Dmitri won the Compass Award competition. His translation of N. Zabolotsky's collection *Columns* is slated for 2023 by Arc Publications.

Michelle Mirabella is a Spanish to English literary translator whose work appears in *The Arkansas International, World Literature Today, Latin American Literature Today, Firmament,* the anthology *Daughters of Latin America* published by HarperCollins in 2023, and elsewhere. She was shortlisted for the 2022 John Dryden Translation Competition and was a finalist in *Columbia Journal*'s Spring 2022 Contest in the translation category. A 2022 ALTA Travel Fellow, Michelle is an alumna of the Banff International Literary Translation Centre and the Bread Loaf Translators' Conference. Find more of her work at www.michellemirabella.com.

Brian Robert Moore is a literary translator from New York. His translations from the Italian include the novels *A Silence Shared* by Lalla Romano and *Verdigris* by Michele Mari, as well as Mari's short story collection *You, Bleeding Childhood*. He has received a National Endowment for the Arts Translation Fellowship, a Santa Maddalena Foundation Fellowship, and the PEN Grant for the English Translation of Italian Literature.

Harry Morales is a Spanish literary translator. His translations include the work of Mario Benedetti, Julio Cortázar, Emir Rodríguez Monegal,

Juan Rulfo, and Ilan Stavans, among many other distinguished writers. His work has been widely anthologized and has appeared in *Kenyon Review*, *The Iowa Review*, *Michigan Quarterly Review*, *Shenandoah*, and *LitMag*, among others. He is the translator of Mario Benedetti's *Only in the Meantime & Office Poems* (Host Publications, 2006), *The Rest is Jungle and Other Stories* (Host Publications, 2010), and *La Tregua*, published as *The Truce: The Diary of Martín Santomé* (Penguin UK Modern Classics, 2015).

Behçet Necatigil (1916–1979), stands outside the main movements of modern Turkish poetry as an original and innovative voice. His early poetry was often narrative and highly atmospheric, but over the years he purged his work of this element and wrote very concentrated, elliptical verse that utilized all the properties of the Turkish language. He also wrote a number of very original radio plays and translated from the German and Persian.

Shoshana Olidort is a writer, critic, and translator. Her work has appeared or is forthcoming in *Asymptote*, *The Los Angeles Review of Books*, *Columbia Journal*, *The Cortland Review*, *Jewish Currents*, *The Laurel Review*, *Lit Hub*, *The New Republic*, *Poetry Northwest*, *The Times Literary Supplement*, and *World Literature Today*, among other outlets. She holds a Ph.D. in comparative literature from Stanford University and is the web editor for the Poetry Foundation.

A writer and scholar, **Gustavo Pérez Firmat** is the David Feinson Professor Emeritus of Humanities at Columbia University. His books of literary and cultural criticism include *Life on the Hyphen*, *The Havana Habit*, *Tongue Ties*, and *The Cuban Condition*.

Farhad Pirbal (born 1961) is an iconic Kurdish writer, poet, painter, critic, singer, and scholar. He has lived in Kurdistan, Iraq, Iran, Syria,

Germany, Denmark, and France, where he obtained his Ph.D. in history of contemporary Kurdish literature at the Sorbonne. Publishing since 1979, Pirbal has authored more than seventy books of poetry, writing, and translation and serves as one of Kurdistan's farthest reaching voices. In 2024, marking his English-language debut, Deep Vellum will publish his collected poems, *Refugee Number 33,333*, and his debut short story collection, *The Potato Eaters*.

Gala Pushkarenko is a heteronym of Oleg Shatybelko, a Russian poet born in 1968. He has published since 2001, worked as a poetry journal executive editor, and is a member of the poetry group Polutona. Oleg is the author of five books of poetry (from 2002 to 2019) and multiple journal and online publications. Since 2018 he has authored five more books as Gala Pushkarenko.

Julia Rendón Abrahamson is the author of the novel *Lengua ajena* (De Conatus, 2022) and the short story collections *Yeguas y terneros* (La Caída Editorial, 2021) and *La casa está muy grande* (Linda y Fatal Ediciones Argentina, 2015). She is a 2021 winner of the Montserrat Roig Grant for Literary Creation from the City Hall of Barcelona under UNESCO's City of Literature program. Rendón Abrahamson is part of the recent "boom" of Ecuadorian women writers reaching the international market. She has degrees from Boston College, Parsons School of Design, the National University of the Arts, Argentina, and Casa de Letras.

Maurice Rodriguez is an emerging writer and translator with an M.A. in English from the University of Connecticut. He's also an M.F.A. student in Creative Writing at The New School where he concentrates in fiction and nonfiction. His latest publications can be found at *ANMLY*, *Puerto del Sol*, and *HASH*. Follow him on X/Twitter for more writing and translating updates @yosoymojo.

Mirza Mohammad Ali Saeb Tabrizi (d. 1592) was the most accomplished Persian poet of his age. The poet laureate of the Safavid court, he spent seven years of his life in voluntary exile at the Mughal courts of India. He is one of the most prolific composers of the ghazal (Persian lyric), with around seventy thousand extant lines of poetry. He is also well known as a distinguished poet of classical Persian poetry's Indian style, which is characterized by elaborate conceits and labyrinthine poetic images.

Menghis Samuel is founder, owner, and managing director of Ewan Technology Solutions, Inc. in Eritrea. A veteran of Eritrea's armed struggle for independence, an engineer, and a designer, he has lived in the United States and worked as a project manager at AT&T. He is Chairman of the Board of the Eritrean National Chamber of Commerce. A poet and translator, his most recent work includes the cotranslation of *Gfi Gezati Ethiopia ab Ertra* ("Atrocities by Ethiopian Rulers in Eritrea").

Poet, playwright, and translator, **Sherod Santos** is the author of seven books of poetry, a book of essays, and a book of translations from the early Greek poets. A National Book Award, New Yorker Book Award, and National Book Critics Award Finalist, he received an Award in Literature from the American Academy of Arts and Letters.

Fatemeh Shams is the author of two books of poetry in Persian, the first of which won the Jaleh Esfahani Award for the best young Iranian poet in 2012, and a critical monograph in English on poetry and politics, *A Revolution in Rhyme* (Oxford UP). *When They Broke Down the Door* (Mage), a collection of her poems translated by Dick Davis, won the 2017 Latifeh Yarshater Award from the Association for Iranian Studies. Her poetry has been featured in the Poetry Foundation website, PBS NewsHour, *World Literature Today*, and the *Penguin Book of*

Feminist Writing, among other venues. She is Associate Professor of Persian Literature at the University of Pennsylvania.

Cynthia Steele is an emerita professor at the University of Washington in Seattle. She has published translations of books by Inés Arredondo, José Emilio Pacheco, and María Gudín. Her work has also appeared in *Michigan Quarterly Review, New England Review, Washington Square Review, Chicago Review*, and *Agni*.

Kayvan Tahmasebian translates poetry from English and French into Persian, and from Persian into English. He is the author of *Lecture on Fear and Other Poems* (Radical Paper Press, 2019). With Rebecca Ruth Gould, he cotranslated *House Arrest: Poems of Hasan Alizadeh* (Arc Publications, 2022), which was awarded a PEN Translates award, and *High Tide of the Eyes: Poems by Bijan Elahi* (Operating System, 2019). His cotranslation of Hormoz Shahdadi's *Night of Terror* was awarded a grant from PEN Presents in 2023. He is the author of *Isfahan's Mold* (Goman Publishers, 2016).

ko ko thett is a Burma-born poet and poetry translator. He has published twelve collections of poetry and translations in both Burmese and English. His poems have been translated into several languages, from Brazilian Portuguese to Finnish, and are widely anthologized. His work has been recognized with a fellowship from the University of Iowa and an English PEN Translates award. ko ko thett's most recent poetry collection is *Bamboophobia* (Zephyr Press, 2022). He lives in Norwich, UK.

Joanna Trzeciak Huss is Professor of Translation Studies at Kent State University. Her translations from Polish and Russian have appeared in *The New York Times, The New Yorker, Times Literary Supplement, Harpers, The Atlantic, Paris Review, Field, Pleiades, The*

Hopkins Review, Zvezda, Boston Review, nonsite, and *New Ohio Review,* among others. Her books of poetry translation include *Miracle Fair: Selected Poems of Wisława Szymborska* (W. W. Norton) and *Sobbing Superpower: Selected Poems of Tadeusz Różewicz* (W. W. Norton). Her *Collected Poems of Zuzanna Ginczanka* is forthcoming from Zephyr Press. She is the recipient of the 2020 Michael Heim Prize for Collegial Translation.

Enrique S. Villasis is a poet and scriptwriter. His first book of poems, *Agua* (Librong Lira, 2015 & 2022) was a finalist for National Book Awards in the Philippines. His second book of poems is forthcoming.

Tesfamariam Woldemariam (1948–2015) joined the Eritrean armed revolution fresh out the University of Asmara in the mid-1970s. He quickly became a leading intellectual, writing in Tigrinya and establishing new Tigrinya journals. Internal conflicts within Eritrea's liberation forced him to immigrate to Sudan in the early 1980s and eventually to the United States. He continued to write poetry and occasionally published essays, but he labored in obscurity, living in Atlanta. In 2014, Hdri Publishers invited him back to Eritrea to create a new collection of his poetry, which confirmed him as Eritrea's greatest modern poet.

Yoo Heekyung is a South Korean poet and playwright. He is the author of the poetry collections *Oneul achim daneo* (Moonji Books, 2011), *Dangsinui jari—namuro jaraneun bangbeop* (achimdalbooks, 2013), *Uriege jamsi sinieotdeon* (Moonji Books, 2018), *Idaeum bome urineun* (achimdalbooks, 2021) and two essay collections. He is a playwright with the theater company dock and a member of the poetry collective jaknan (作亂). In 2019, Yoo was awarded the Hyundae Munhak Sang (Contemporary Literature Award) for his poetry. He runs wit n cynical, a poetry bookstore and project space in Seoul.

Mona Zaki obtained her doctorate in Near Eastern Studies from Princeton University in 2015. She currently teaches Arabic and Middle East Literature at William & Mary in Virginia. She was a contributing editor, reviewer, and translator for *Banipal: Journal in Arabic Literature* from 1999–2013. She translated a debut novel of the Libyan Mansour Bushnaf, *Chewing Gum,* in 2017.

PREVIOUS PUBLICATIONS

We gratefully acknowledge the editors of the journals who first selected these translations for publication.

ANMLY: "Bird-women"
Another Chicago Magazine: "00572"
The Antonym: "Bone"
Asymptote: "First We'll Speak Many Words About God"; *Unstill Life with Cat* (excerpt)
AzonaL: "Water_Miniatures: Unboxing"
Columbia Journal: "A Body"
Consequence: "The Snail's Spiral"
Copper Nickel: "[I have a collection of powerful objects]"
Firmament: "Family Portrait of the Black Earth"
The Gettysburg Review: "Grazing Land"
Guernica: "Our Village"
The Hopkins Review: "Joyful Mythology"
LARB: "Deterioration" and "A Red Blight"
LitMag: "Bottle to the Sea (Epilogue to a Story)"
The Margins: "[Untitled]"
The Markaz Review: "Settling: Toward an Arabic Translation of the English Word 'Home'"
The Massachusetts Review: "Graceless"
MAYDAY: "We Will Survive"
Michigan Quarterly Review: "Death, Peppermint Flavoured," "The Reeling City"

New England Review: *Guerrilla Blooms* (excerpt)
North American Review: "In the Meantime /Mientras llega"
POETRY: "A Hymn to Ra," "Rune Poems from Bergen, Norway, Thirteenth and Fourteenth Century"
Poetry Northwest: "Deterioration"
The Southern Review: "Neighbor"
Tupelo Quarterly: "The mistress of the house"
Two Lines: "The Funeral"
Washington Square Review: "Sea Krait"
Words Without Borders: "Near the Shrine of Saint Naum"
World Literature Today: Two Mapuche-Huilliche Poems
Your Impossible Voice: "The Lion"

NOTABLE TRANSLATIONS PUBLISHED IN 2022

Arranged by translator's last name, these translations are those that were longlisted for inclusion in this edition of Best Literary Translations.

- From *Guerrilla Blooms* by Daniela Catrileo, translated by Edith Adams (*mercury firs*)
- "Meat Grinder" by Milad Kamyabian, translated by Ali Asadollahi (*Hayden's Ferry Review*)
- From "Collapse" (parts 3–11) by Elsa Cross, translated by Susan Ayres (*Northwest Review*)
- "The Canal" by Sabahattin Ali, translated by Aysel K. Basci (*The Los Angeles Review*)
- "Men Wound in Shrouds of Silence" by Tahar Ben Jelloun, translated by Conor Bracken (Action Books blog)
- "Siri, My Love; Zuckerbook, My Home" by Mose Njo, translated by Allison M. Charette (*Future Science Fiction Digest*)
- "Standing at the Empty Mouth" by Abboud Aljabiri, translated by Jeffrey Clapp and Muntather Alsawad (*MAYDAY*)
- "And I Loved the Boys" by Muhammad ibn Dāniyāl, translated by Alex de Voogt (*The Ilanot Review*)
- "Notes on 'The Scream'" by Edvard Munch, translated by Eirill Alvilde Falck (*Poetry*)
- "Glass" by Rema Hmoud, translated by Ibrahim Fawzy (*ArabLit Quarterly*)

- Selections from *Night* by Ennio Moltedo, translated by Marguerite Feitlowitz (*World Poetry Review*)
- "A Burning Crossword Puzzle" by Ksenia Buksha, translated by Anne O. Fisher (*Consequence*)
- "An Artist's Ego" by Shagufta Sharmeen Tania, translated by Torsa Ghosal (*The Massachusetts Review*)
- "To Kill a Fly" by Mariela Dreyfus, translated by Carmen Giménez and Zachary Payne (*AGNI*)
- "Divorce 2" by Tove Ditlevsen, translated by Cynthia Graae (*The Ilanot Review*)
- "The Words of the Old and the Young" by Tristan Tzara, translated by Heather Green (*AGNI*)
- "Insurgentes" by Claudina Domingo, translated by Ryan Greene (*Quarterly West*)
- "In Heat" by Gabriel Carle, translated by Heather Houde (*The Common*)
- "*Komono Ichiran*, or The Possibilities of an Atom" by Megumi Andrade Kobayashi, translated by Will Howard (*The Offing*)
- "They were singing a folk song . . . " "And had you asked me how it feels—" "Not long is left until a kiss and the spring . . . " "When they dragged him out of the school yard . . . " by Kateryna Kalytko, translated by Olena Jennings and Oksana Lutsyshyna (*Two Lines*)
- "We woke up at 5:00 A.M.," by Anastasia Afanasieva, translated by Ilya Kaminsky and Katie Ferris (*World Literature Today*)
- "Set Change" by Yuri Andrukhovych, translated by Ostap Kin and John Hennessy (*New York Review of Books*)
- "How to enter the Vatnajökull Glacier and Survive with a Mouthful of Comet's Breath" by Rocío Cerón, translated by Dallin Law (*Denver Quarterly*)
- "My Fur Rabbit" by Hon Lai-chu, translated by Jacqueline Leung (*Nashville Review*)

- "In Luxor: The Poet on Vacation" by Saadi Youssef, translated by Khaled Mattawa (*Michigan Quarterly Review*)
- "Couper Les Tiges" by Virginie Lalucq, translated by Claire McQuerry and Céline Bourhis (*Denver Quarterly*)
- "Chess Piece" by Natalia García Freire, translated by Michelle Mirabella (*The Arkansas International*)
- Selections from *Yidishe Dikhterins* by Hinde Roytblat and Dina Libkes, translated by Reyzl Grace MoChridhe (*In geveb*)
- "The Levy" by Khane Levin, translated by Reyzl Grace MoChridhe (*Alchemy*)
- "Gestation" by Mariana Travacio, translated by Will Morningstar (*Two Lines*)
- "Score for Fish Choir" by Riva Palacio Obón, translated by Will Morningstar (*ANMLY*)
- "STRATEGhIC PLANeING" by Andrés Ajens, translated by Erín Moure (Action Books Blog)
- "The Last Wolf of Ireland" by Dan Murphy, translated by Dan Murphy (*Terrain*)
- "Ropes" by Claudia Peña Claros, translated by Robin Myers (*Latin American Literature Today*)
- "Twilight" by Louisa Siefert, translated by Laura Nagle (*Circumference*)
- "Wild Song" by Antonia Pozzi, translated by Amy Newman (*The Ilanot Review*)
- "For the Next Instant's I" by Kim Hyesoon, translated by Cindy Juyoung Ok (*Hayden's Ferry Review*)
- "With My Brother on My Mind" by Kim Hoyeonjae, translated by Suphil Lee Park (*The Cincinnati Review*)
- "To My Youth, Good Riddance" by María Mercedes Carranza, translated by Jere Paulmeno (*Another Chicago Magazine*)
- "I Like to Kiss Scars" by Rosa Chávez, translated by Gabriela Ramírez-Chávez (*Poetry*)

- "A Practical Guide for Those Who Want to Write as Little as Possible" by Paolo Albani, translation by Jamie Richards (*Firmament*)
- "I Suppose" by Leila Guerriero, translated by Frances Riddle (*The Southern Review*)
- "Blood-Red Sweat/Lal Pasina" by Abhimanyu Unnuth, translated by Rashi Rohatgi (*World Literature Today*)
- "Imprisoned Words" by Alireza Nouri, translated by Marjan Modarres Sabzevari (*Denver Quarterly*)
- "The Missing Island" by Estelle Coppolani, translated by Vasantha Sambamurti (*Copihue Poetry*)
- "Witness" by Fabio Pusterla, translated by Will Schutt (*The Arkansas International*)
- "Lake Balaton" by Csenger Kertai, translated by Diana Senechal (*Literary Imagination*)
- "The bombing" by Milena Marković, translated by Steven Teref and Maja Teref (*Exchanges*)
- "Brigitte Bardot" by Milena Marković, translated by Steven Teref and Maja Teref (*Tupelo Quarterly*)
- "Truro" by Julien Gracq, translated by Alice Yang (*AGNI*)
- "The Year of Ukraine" by Iya Kiva, translated by Katherine E. Young (*Los Angeles Review of Books*)

GUEST EDITOR BIOGRAPHY

Jane Hirshfield is the author of ten much-honored collections of poetry and two now-classic books of essays, *Nine Gates* (HarperCollins, 1997) and *Ten Windows* (Knopf, 2015). Her cotranslation with Mariko Aratani, *The Ink Dark Moon: Love Poems by Ono no Komachi and Izumi Shikibu, Women of the Ancient Japanese Court* (Vintage Classics, 1990), received Columbia University's Translation Center Award and has been continuously in print for thirty years. She has also written a best-selling ebook, *The Heart of Haiku*, edited *Women in Praise of the Sacred: 43 Centuries of Spiritual Poetry by Women* (HarperCollins, 1994), and cotranslated, with Robert Bly, *Mirabai: Ecstatic Poems* (Beacon Press, 2004). Hirshfield's honors include fellowships from the Guggenheim and Rockefeller Foundations and the National Endowment for the Arts, the Poetry Center Book Award, California Book Award, and longlist/finalist listing for the National Book Award, the National Book Critics Circle Award, and England's T. S. Eliot Prize in Poetry. A former chancellor of the Academy of American Poets and elected member of the American Academy of Arts and Sciences, Hirshfield's poems and essays have been translated into seventeen languages. *The Asking: New & Selected Poems* appeared from Knopf in fall 2023.

SERIES COEDITORS' BIOGRAPHIES

Noh Anothai has translated both classical Siamese poets and contemporary Thai authors, including recipients of the Southeast Asian Writers (SEAWrite) award, for journals like *Asymptote*, *Two Lines*, and *World Literature Today*. In 2016, his *Poems from the Buddha's Footprint* (Singing Bone Press) became the first full-length translation of a work by the celebrated early Bangkok poet Sunthorn Phu published outside of Thailand. Profiled in *The Nikkei Asian Review* and *Prestige Thailand* for his work as a translator, Anothai has also taught creative writing in the U.S. and in Thailand, lectured at the Siam Society under royal patronage, and served as a judge for the Lucien Stryk Prize for Asian Literature in Translation. He holds a Ph.D. in comparative literature from Washington University in St. Louis.

Wendy Call is author of *No Word for Welcome*, winner of the Grub Street National Book Prize for Nonfiction, and the chapbook *Tilled Paths Through Wilds of Thought*. She is also coeditor of the craft anthology *Telling True Stories*, translator of two books of poems by Irma Pineda, and cotranslator of a poetry collection by Mikeas Sánchez. Her creative nonfiction has appeared in many journals, including *The Georgia Review*, *Lit Hub*, *StoryQuarterly*, *Witness*, and *World Literature Today*. She was a 2015 National Endowment for the Arts Fellow in Poetry Translation, a 2019 Fulbright Faculty Scholar in Colombia, and, in 2023, Distinguished Visiting Writer at Cornell College and Translator in Residence at the University of Iowa.

Öykü **Tekten** is a poet, translator, editor, and archivist living between Granada and New York. She is also a founding member of Pinsapo, a New York-based collective and press with a particular focus on work in and about translation, as well as a contributing editor and archivist with Lost & Found: The CUNY Poetics Document Initiative. Her work has appeared in the *Academy of American Poets, Poetry, Words Without Borders, FENCE*, and *World Literature Today* among other places. She is the translator of *Selected Poems* by Betül Dünder (Belladonna* Collaborative, 2023) and the cotranslator of *Separated from the Sun* by İlhan Sami Çomak (Smokestack Books, 2022).

Kọ́lá Túbọ̀sún is the publisher of *OlongoAfrica*. He is the author of two collections of poetry, *Edwardsville by Heart* (2018) and *Ìgbà Èwe* (2021), and an online dictionary of Yorùbá names. He is a Fulbright Scholar (2009) and a Chevening Research Fellow at the British Library in London (2019/2020). His work has been published in *African Writer, Aké Review, Brittle Paper, International Literary Quarterly, Enkare Review, Maple Tree Literary Supplement, Jalada, Popula, Saraba Magazine*, etc. He has translated works of Chimamanda Adichie, Haruki Murakami, Ngũgĩ wa Thiong'o, Wole Soyinka, James Baldwin, Sarah Ladipo-Manyika, Cervantes, and others between English and Yorùbá. His work in language advocacy earned him the Premio Ostana Special Prize in 2016. He shares his time between Lagos and Minnesota.

Printed in the USA
CPSIA information can be obtained
at www.ICGtesting.com
JSHW022157250224
58033JS00002B/2